Luke stopped and turned towards her.

His face and his body were in shadow but Kate could feel his presence as clearly as if it were day. Gently he pulled her towards him so that their bodies were touching, as closely as they had been in their one dance. 'I don't know you very well,' she said tremulously.

'How long does it take?' His arms wrapped round her, tightened, and he stooped his head towards her. Kate sighed, a great breath of anticipation, and tilted her head backwards so her face was raised to his. For an eternal moment she felt as if they were fused into one, tied by the sweetness of a kiss. Of one thing she was certain. She'd never felt like this before.

Kids. . .one of life's joys, one of life's treasures.

Kisses. . .of warmth, kisses of passion, kisses from mothers and kisses from lovers.

In *Kids & Kisses*. . .every story has it all.

Gill Sanderson is a psychologist who finds time to write only by staying up late at night. Weekends are filled by her hobbies of gardening, running and mountain walking. Her ideas come from her work, from one son who is an oncologist, one son who is a nurse and her daughter, who is a trainee midwife. She first wrote articles for learned journals and chapters for a textbook. Then she was encouraged to change to fiction by her husband, who is an established writer of war stories.

Recent titles by the same author:

COUNTRY DOCTORS

DR RYDER
AND SON

BY
GILL SANDERSON

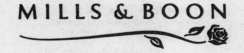

DID YOU PURCHASE THIS BOOK WITHOUT A COVER?
If you did, you should be aware it is **stolen property** as it was reported *unsold and destroyed* by a retailer. Neither the Author nor the publisher has received any payment for this book.

All the characters in this book have no existence outside the imagination of the author, and have no relation whatsoever to anyone bearing the same name or names. They are not even distantly inspired by any individual known or unknown to the author, and all the incidents are pure invention.

All rights reserved including the right of reproduction in whole or in part in any form. This edition is published by arrangement with Harlequin Enterprises II B.V. The text of this publication or any part thereof may not be reproduced or transmitted in any form or by any means, electronic or mechanical, including photocopying, recording, storage in an information retrieval system, or otherwise, without the written permission of the publisher.

This book is sold subject to the condition that it shall not, by way of trade or otherwise, be lent, resold, hired out or otherwise circulated without the prior consent of the publisher in any form of binding or cover other than that in which it is published and without a similar condition including this condition being imposed on the subsequent purchaser.

MILLS & BOON, the Rose Device and
LOVE ON CALL are trademarks of the publisher.
Harlequin Mills & Boon Limited,
Eton House, 18-24 Paradise Road, Richmond, Surrey TW9 1SR

© Gill Sanderson 1996

ISBN 0 263 79765 1

Set in Times 10 on $10^1/_2$pt. by
Rowland Phototypesetting Limited
Bury St Edmunds, Suffolk

03-9608-52833

Made and printed in Great Britain

CHAPTER ONE

THE white-coated doctor smiled at the figure lying on the bed and said, 'You're a sister, aren't you? I don't know whether medical people are better or worse patients.'

Kate Storm smiled back. 'I could be prejudiced, but I think nurses make good patients and doctors make bad.'

'That's entirely possible. Doctors don't like to think they're vulnerable, even to disease. Now, how's the local anaesthetic working? Any feeling there at all?' The doctor turned to his trolley.

'It all feels quite numb.'

'Good. Now, I know you know what we're going to do but you don't want to watch, do you?'

Kate shook her head, and the nurse hovering in the background carefully erected a little screen immediately below her chin. Kate could just see the doctor's head as he bent over.

There was no pain but a vague feeling of pressure on her sternum and then a jerk as the needle broke through. She knew what was happening; as a cancer nurse she'd assisted at this many times herself. Perhaps it was a good thing for a nurse to be a patient once in a while.

The doctor was thrusting a needle into her breastbone and drawing out a sample of bone marrow. He wouldn't have enough for any kind of therapy, but just enough so that her marrow could be typed.

Increasingly, patients with leukaemia were being given allogeneic transplants—healthy marrow injected into them from a donor. But finding a suitable donor was often difficult; bone marrow wasn't as easy to match as blood.

'Right, Miss Storm, we've finished.' The doctor's

6 DR RYDER AND SON

smiling face reappeared. 'When this has been typed it'll be entered on our database. I don't need to tell you that there's only a small chance of our wanting to harvest your bone marrow. But it's good of you to volunteer. Someday you may help someone who desperately needs what only you can give.'

'I'm happy to do it,' she said. But later, as she walked away from the clinic, it struck her that she didn't really feel pleased about what she had done. She felt indifferent.

She was tired—not physically but spiritually. It wasn't as bad as the complete burn-out suffered by some, and it could happen to any nurse. But a nurse working in a paediatric cancer ward was more at risk than most. Sister Kate Storm had thought that she was on top of her job. She had thought that she was mistress of the necessary combination of sympathy and detached professionalism. It seemed that she might have been wrong.

It had crept up on her gradually. No longer did she have the same sense of joy when she walked onto Aladdin Ward. She didn't have the same feeling of satisfaction at the end of each shift. She'd made one or two tiny mistakes—nothing important, of course, but it was worrying. And her personal life—well, she didn't really have one. The hospital was her life.

It was half past three in the afternoon and one of those rare quiet times when she felt happy taking a rest. Her patients were settled and comfortable, her staff had jobs that they could cope with, her paperwork was finished. She poured herself a coffee and sat in her office easy chair. Bliss! For fifteen minutes she could close her eyes and think of nothing.

Of course, someone had to tap on the office door. 'Come in,' she called, half surprised at the sharpness of her voice and the unreasoning annoyance that flooded through her. But, after all, this was the first real break she'd had all day.

GILL SANDERSON

Then her face cleared as a middle-aged man with spiky grey hair and half-moon glasses popped his head round the door. 'Mike!' she exclaimed. 'I thought you'd finished for the day.'

'I wanted to come back to see my favourite ward sister. I need a favour.'

Dr Mike Hamilton, consultant oncologist on Kate's ward, walked into the office. 'I don't suppose there's a spare coffee for me?'

'Of course!' Kate moved to stand up but Mike put a reassuring hand on her shoulder and pressed her down again.

'Don't get up. Everything's quiet on the Western Front outside. I'll pour my own and we'll sit here and have a pleasant and civilised chat.'

She relaxed into her chair with a sigh as Mike filled a mug and looked mournfully in her biscuit tin. 'Chocolate digestives are in the drawer,' she said. 'I bought you another packet.'

'You're the perfect nurse. You anticipate my every need—be it scalpel, suture or chocolate digestive biscuit.'

Kate smiled. 'Every nurse on this ward knows the way to your heart is through a packet of biscuits.'

'It's sad to be so transparent,' he said, opening the packet with precise, surgeon's movements. 'But on the other hand it has its good points.'

He sat opposite her and for a while there was a companionable silence between them. All the staff on Aladdin Ward called each other by their Christian names. They thought of themselves as a team, with each member's contribution being valuable and recognised. Kate knew how much of this camaraderie came from Mike's leadership.

'What is this favour you want?' she asked after a while.

He looked slightly sheepish. 'This morning I checked the nursing roster. Apparently you're off on Friday.'

DR RYDER AND SON

She nodded. 'It's my long weekend.'

'Have you got any plans? Going away, visiting anybody?'

Shaking her head, she said, 'Nothing planned at all. Why?'

'I've got Sally Vincent coming back in—complete with family, of course. You're the only person I know who can handle them.'

Kate tried to suppress a grin. It was nice that the Vincent family doted on eight-year-old Sally. Unfortunately they did so loudly and emotionally. It often took all her persuasive powers to ensure that there was just a little peace near Sally's bed. Then she calculated and the smile slipped. 'Sally's not due back in for treatment for another month.'

'She's had a relapse,' Mike said bleakly. 'It doesn't look good.'

'I see.' Kate remembered the solemn little girl. She had A.M.L.—acute myeloid leukaemia. It had seemed to respond well to treatment—but no treatment was ever certain.

'There's no problem,' she said to Mike. 'I'm sure I'll be able to swap with Denise Cowley.'

'Thanks, Kate. I truly appreciate it.'

But even as he spoke Kate was conscious of a lowering of her spirits. She could have done with a full three days' break. She loved her work; she knew that she was good at it. But recently it had seemed to stretch in front of her with no possible end.

'How old are you, Kate?'

It was a personal question, but Mike was a friend; he was entitled to ask.

'I'll be twenty-six in a couple of months.'

'Sometimes, when you close your eyes, you look older.'

Now, that was hurtful. But she knew that Mike was a kind and considerate person. He went on, 'You live in a hospital flat. And you've worked on this ward for the past two years.'

'Yes.' Kate felt uneasy. She didn't know where these questions were leading.

'How long since you had a fortnight's holiday—say in Spain or somewhere like that?'

'I've never been abroad. But last summer I had four days walking in the Lake District,' she said defensively. 'Anyway, I don't need holidays. The hospital is my life.'

'Quite. And before you started on this ward two years ago you had an unpaid year's leave of absence. You stayed at home to nurse your father. He died of lung cancer.'

'My father brought me up after my mother died,' Kate said thinly. 'He made sacrifices. What I did for him was little enough.'

'So after he died you wanted to do more. You applied to work on a paediatric cancer ward—possibly the toughest kind of nursing there is.'

Kate had had enough. She snapped, 'I don't see the point of these questions, Mike, and I don't like them. My personal life is my own. Let's keep it that way.'

He smiled gently. 'When I first saw you on the ward I wondered if you'd last. You had your arms round a little girl who was crying, and you looked near to tears yourself. You so obviously felt for her that I thought you'd never be able to take the pain that this job can bring. But that sweet face of yours is deceptive, Kate. There's steel underneath. I think you're probably the most competent nurse I've ever worked with.'

It was a rare compliment and she appreciated it. But she still felt apprehensive. 'What are you getting at, Mike?'

He paused before answering and then said simply, 'Sometimes you look exhausted.'

That was ridiculous. With a short laugh she said, 'Sometimes we all look exhausted. But I'm the hospital ladies' squash champion. I swim four times a week. I

10 DR RYDER AND SON

eat well and I sleep well. If every nurse was as fit as me there would be fewer days lost through illness.'

'There's exhaustion of the spirit as well as the body, Kate.' When she made no answer he went on, 'Is there any special man in your life?'

Now this was too much. She was about to tell him angrily that it was none of his business when he lifted a defensive hand and said, 'Please answer, Kate. You know I've got your best interests at heart.'

Gruffly she said, 'There's no man in my life, special or otherwise. I wish I could say there was but I just never seem to meet the right sort.'

'I see. The reason I—' There was a sudden muted buzz. From his pocket Mike took his pager and looked at it in disgust. However, he was a professional. Kate passed him the telephone and listened to the kind of conversation she heard so often.

'Yes. . . He's what? Look, it's probably nothing but I think I'll come and have a look anyway. . . You have the X-rays? I'll be there in five minutes.'

Hastily he swallowed the rest of his coffee and grabbed another chocolate biscuit. 'Mother Goose Ward,' he muttered to Kate. 'Dr Norman has a problem—again.' It was rather unprofessional of him to say that but Kate knew exactly what he meant. Dr Arthur Norman was the one piece of grit in a smooth-running machine.

'Look, Kate,' Mike went on, 'I want to have a serious talk with you some time soon.'

'I'm all right,' she said soothingly. 'Don't worry about me.'

'I do,' he said, and left.

A second later the door opened again and his head popped through. 'I completely forgot to mention it,' he gasped. 'Got an old friend dropping in tomorrow. Name's Ryder. If he gets here before me, make him comfortable.' The door slammed a second time. Something sparked in her memory but she couldn't think what.

Kate poured herself another coffee and noticed that her hand was shaking slightly. Mike's comments must have upset her more than she'd realised. It was good of him to think about her—but, of course, his ideas were completely wrong.

As ever, she was late leaving the ward. She had to hand over to Mary Castle, the night sister, and they seemed to spend quite a time discussing their patients.

After a light meal in the canteen she went back to her room and read for a while. She found that reading the necessary nursing and medical magazines kept her up to date. There were a couple of ideas on nursing care that she thought she'd bring up with Mike.

At eight that night she had a squash match. She changed into her whites, walked down to the gym and had three hard, fast games. Afterwards she had a single glass of white wine in the bar and an hour's hospital gossip with her colleagues. Then to bed. As usual, it had been a full day. Just before she went to sleep she thought about Mike Hamilton's warning. It was nice of him to be concerned about her, but he was wrong.

Next morning she wasn't so sure. She woke early and lay in bed for a while, her eyes wandering round the hospital room that was her home. It was comfortable enough and there were personal touches—books, pictures, flowers—to make it individual. But basically it was just a hospital room, pleasant but characterless.

She showered and dressed. It was felt that the children who were their patients might be a little overawed by the traditional nurses' uniform so Kate wore a pastel smock with pictures of elephants and giraffes.

Before she left for breakfast she checked her appearance in the mirror. Did she look exhausted? Her body, she knew, looked well. She had been born slim and long-legged and exercise had kept her trim and supple. The smock she wore hinted at the generous feminine

12 DR RYDER AND SON

curves of breast, waist and hip. Her body was fine.

What about her face? She sighed. There was a saying that your face is your fortune, but too often Kate's face had been her misfortune. Her dark hair she now kept cut short; it was neat and convenient. Sometimes she wished that her face could be as practical. But it wasn't. Wide eyes and ready smiling lips made her look sweet, guileless and totally innocent. Children were attracted to her. So were men, but they tended to think that her naïve expression somehow reflected her character. It didn't.

Kate sighed again. Perhaps she was getting a little cynical. Her experiences with men hadn't tended to be happy. And perhaps there were faint fatigue lines round the corners of her eyes.

After breakfast she walked briskly over to Aladdin Ward. There were the usual routine tasks and then, in the middle of the morning, a new child to be admitted. Jamie Bartlett, a woebegone seven-year-old, clutched his mother with one hand and his teddy with the other. His parents looked as white-faced as Jamie did.

The family was met and welcomed by Judith Doyle, the senior registrar, with Kate discreetly in attendance. The first few minutes were all important. If a child could be made to feel comfortable and happy in the little ward, then the treatment would be so much easier. Jamie's mother was going to stay with him; she also had to be reassured.

While Judith took the parents for a coffee and a chat to explain what was happening Kate took Jamie's hand and showed him round. This was where she excelled. Children automatically liked and trusted her. She helped Jamie into his pyjamas, stuck his pictures on the wall and tucked Teddy up into bed. Then she stayed chatting until Judith came.

Jamie had already had a blood count and his white-cell count was so high that his GP was practically certain that he had leukaemia. However, a bone-marrow test would offer more information and determine whether he was suffering from lymphoblastic leukaemia or the rarer and more dangerous myeloid form.

Judith started the long induction process. While Kate kept Jamie's attention she carefully inserted a needle with a plastic tube attached into one of the veins on the back of Jamie's hand. Then she withdrew the needle so that the catheter was in place for any drips or injections that might be needed. This was the first hurdle. Jamie's lip trembled because it was quite a painful injection, but he didn't cry. Both Judith and Kate felt relieved.

The rest of the battery of tests followed quickly. There were measurements of height and weight, specimens and swabs to be taken, temperature, pulse, blood pressure, a trip to have his chest X-rayed. His blood was tested twice. And all the time Kate had to reconcile the necessity of the tests with the fact that Jamie was a half-terrified small boy. It was absorbing, rewarding work but it was physically and emotionally draining.

Finally they were finished. Jamie was dozing in his new bed and a slightly reassured mother was lying on her bed nearby, watching as if the very intensity of her gaze would help cure her son. Kate took Judith back to the office for a coffee.

'Thanks, Kate. I don't know how, but you seem to make the work go easier. I wish all the nurses had your touch with the kids.'

Kate shrugged. 'It's just a question of taking time. If they know and trust you. . .no trouble.'

'You make it sound simple. I've got two kids of my own and I know it's not. Anyway. . .' Judith yawned and stretched '. . .I've got somebody to see over on Mother Goose Ward. Thanks again. I'll be along to see young Jamie later.' She left, her pink gown swirling around her.

Kate sneaked a look at her watch. Lunchtime already! She hadn't time to eat; she'd grab a sandwich later.

The work of the ward went on. There were treatments, observations, a young student nurse to be watched and

14 DR RYDER AND SON

guided. It was early afternoon before Kate felt that she could treat herself to the long-promised egg and cress sandwich.

It was turning into a typical day—hard work but satisfying, and everything going more or less smoothly. Except. . . Kate frowned. Around her were the sounds of the hospital, so familiar that they weren't even noticed. There was the rattle of feet on the corridor floor, the buzz of conversations, the rattle of cups and the ting of the lift arriving. But something else. In the distance was an angrily raised voice—not a TV programme, she felt sure. Who was shouting on her ward?

Outside her office door the shouting was louder. 'And I tell you she's my daughter and I *am* going in there!' There was some kind of low-voiced reply. Angrily, Kate hurried down the corridor and turned the corner to see what was happening.

The scene was taking place outside one of the little rooms opening off the central corridor. Jenny Metcalfe, the student nurse, was standing red-faced and defiant with her back to the door. Facing her was a large, bearded man, dressed in a donkey jacket, with a large paper parcel incongruously under one arm.

As Kate walked rapidly towards the couple she heard Jenny say, 'I'm sorry, sir, but this is a sterile room and you can't go in without permission. Why don't you wait and talk to one of the doctors?'

'I've waited long enough. Now just get out of the way and there'll be no trouble.'

As Kate drew nearer she could smell the beer on the man's breath, and as he turned to look at her she recognised the glassy look in his eyes. The man was drunk. As if she didn't have enough problems!

Quickly she placed herself beside Jenny, between the man and the door. In what she hoped was a suitably cold voice she said, 'I am Sister Storm, in charge of this ward. Please keep your voice down; there are sick children here.'

The man looked nonplussed at this chilly welcome. Kate turned to Jenny and said, 'All right, Nurse Metcalfe, I'll deal with this gentleman now.' With a surprised look, Jenny scurried away.

They were outside the room occupied by a little girl called Jean Stock. She had been brought in by her mother, frightened like all of the parents who came here, who explained that the father was away working on an oil rig in the North Sea. Jean had been in for some time now; she was very weak. Her treatment was well advanced; she would be vulnerable to any infection.

Kate hoped that she could explain this to the truculent father. Trying to adopt a reasonable tone, she said, 'Mr Stock? We appreciate your concern but it's not a good idea for you to visit just at the moment. Jean is—'

'She's my daughter and I'm going to see her. I've got rights, you know. I can take her out of here if I want and you can't stop me. Doesn't look like you're doing her much good; you can come and see her at home.'

Kate flinched. This man was far more drunk than she'd realised, and totally incapable of listening to reason. But she had to persevere.

'I'm sure you only want what's best for her, Mr Stock, and that's what we're trying to give. If you'd like to come to my office we could have a coffee and—'

'I don't want coffee; I want to see my daughter. And I'm going to!'

He lurched forward and Kate winced at the thought of him crashing into the drips or the monitors surrounding his daughter. Jean was in the last few days of chemotherapy. To avoid infection Mike had suggested reverse barrier nursing. Nothing possibly infectious was allowed near Jean.

Kate tried to reason again. 'The consultant should be here any minute now, Mr Stock, and he'll be able to explain to you. . .'

He stepped closer to her, his hand reaching for the doorhandle. Kate could smell the beer and sweat on him,

16 DR RYDER AND SON

see the grime on his collar. 'I'll talk to the consultant fellow when I've talked to my daughter. And you can't stop me!'

Kate's determination to remain cool and professional snapped. 'Oh, yes, I can! This is my ward and you *won't* interfere with it!'

This was fighting talk—perhaps not the best way to tackle things. He stumbled forward and grabbed her round the waist, throwing her so that her side crashed agonisingly into the doorhandle. Through the pain she wondered what to do next. A scream would probably work but she wasn't prepared to risk her dignity or alarm the ward. Perhaps she could stamp on his foot or even knee him in the groin. Gasping because of the pain, she said, 'You are not to—'

'I think it best if we discuss this quietly.'

From somewhere another man had appeared. Kate had a quick glimpse of a dark suit, of size and authority, of a frowning face. But her attention was all on Mr Stock who had now completely lost control. 'You mind your own business,' he snarled, and reached out a thick arm to grab Kate by the front of her smock.

The stranger's movement was faster. He seized the arm and pulled it backwards. For a moment the two strained, locked still, and then Mr Stock's arm was forced down by his side.

The stranger's voice was calm as he asked, 'Do you want it on your conscience that you killed your own child? That's what you'd be risking if you entered that room. What would your wife say?'

Abruptly the fight left the man. There was one last, blustering attempt at hanging onto his dignity. 'Only the best is good enough for my Jean. I can pay for it!'

'We're trying to do the best for Jean. That's why you can't see her now.'

Mr Stock's wrist was released and he rubbed it with his other hand. Kate realised that it must have taken considerable strength to hold him still so effortlessly.

GILL SANDERSON 17

'I've brought her a doll. It was the best in the shop.'

'I'm sure she'll love it. Now, why don't you bring it back later when you've had a word with your wife? Should I get a porter to find you a taxi?'

'Yes. . . I'll go home now.'

The stranger turned to Kate and lifted his eyebrows. She slipped down the corridor, to find an anxious Jenny hurrying towards her, accompanied by a porter. There was a quick explanation and within a minute the now abject Mr Stock was being shepherded out of the building by the porter. Kate thought that she saw the sheen of tears in his eyes.

'You did well there, Jenny,' Kate complimented the student nurse. 'I'm afraid upset parents are one of the hazards of this job. But they're not usually so drunk.'

'Are you all right, Sister?'

'I think Sister may have bruised her side. She could certainly do with a coffee.'

Things had been happening too fast for Kate. She had been concerned only with the welfare of her patient, the smooth running of the ward. First she told Jenny that she was all right and to carry on with her routine duties. Then at last she looked at the man who, she knew, had dealt with a situation that she hadn't been able to cope with.

It appeared that he was used to taking charge. She began to say, 'I really must thank you, Mr. . .er. . .' when he took her arm and urged her gently down the corridor.

'I think five minutes' rest and a warm drink, don't you? Your office is this way? I saw you wince when you banged against the door, but I don't think you've cracked a rib.'

His voice was soft and its very quietness gave it an air of authority. This was a man who expected people to listen when he spoke. It was also deep, and she thought that she could detect the vaguest hint of a northern accent. Unresisting, she allowed herself to be guided

18   DR RYDER AND SON

along the corridor. 'In here?' She was taken into her own room.

'I see there's the ever present coffee-machine,' he said as he headed her towards the easy chair. 'I'd guess white——and just this time you'd better have sugar. May I pour myself one?'

'Please do,' she said. She felt bewildered. No one had ever taken control of her so completely and so quickly. Perhaps the bruise to her side had affected her more than she'd realised.

She sipped the coffee handed to her and for a moment there was silence as she looked at him with frank curiosity.

Her first, fleeting impressions had been correct. He was black-haired, tall, broad-shouldered. Even as he sat opposite her, perfectly still, there was an air about him of controlled strength. She wasn't in the least surprised that he'd had no trouble with the bear-like Mr Stock.

His lightweight suit was a sombre charcoal hue. His white shirt had the sheen and texture that she knew could only come from silk. Fancifully she thought that all his outfit needed was one of the brightly coloured ties so popular among men at the moment, but this man's tie was black and knitted.

There was something else, something missing. . .she couldn't quite work it out and then it struck her. She'd never seen him smile. His dark eyes remained cold and assessing; the well-cut mouth remained still.

It was time to take charge again. She was Sister Kate Storm and this was her ward. 'I'm sorry about that little scene,' she said. 'We try to arrange counselling for our parents but Mr Stock has been away working. It was just his natural feelings as a parent coming through.'

'I'd sympathise with his natural feelings as a parent if he hadn't been drunk,' the stranger said. 'There was no excuse for behaving the way he did.'

'Perhaps I dealt with him the wrong way?' Kate offered.

GILL SANDERSON 19

'No. You dealt with him well. I was very impressed.'

The compliment was delivered flatly and she felt irritated. Who was this man to tell her how well she was doing her job? Yes, who was he and what was he doing on her ward? He was a disturbing man.

'I'm afraid I don't know your name,' she said. 'Have you come to visit one of the children?'

'No. I've come to see Mike Hamilton but I think I'm a bit early. My name is Luke Ryder.'

The minute he spoke she remembered—not only that Mike had said that he'd be dropping in but where she'd heard the name before. 'Luke Ryder. You're an oncologist at one of the big London hospitals. I read an article by you about palliative care of patients with AIDS and cancer.'

He looked at her thoughtfully. 'I've left London now and I don't do quite as much AIDS work as I did. That article was a bit specialised. Did Mike tell you about it?'

She shook her head. 'No. It's not only doctors that read medical journals, Dr Ryder. Nurses, too, like to keep abreast of new developments.'

He seemed unmoved by her rebuff. 'Some nurses do, but by no means all. Now, how's the side? Would you like me to look at it?'

The very idea made her shiver; she wasn't sure why. 'No, thank you. It's just a bruise; I've had far worse before.'

'As you wish. I. . .'

The door rattled and opened; she looked up. It took an effort not to let the annoyance show on her face but somehow she managed it. Technically this was her office, and though all of the doctors were welcome in it they all recognised that it was her domain. All except for Dr Arthur Norman, that was.

He was the most junior house doctor but was obviously expecting to go far. He was short, round-faced, with a large moustache which Kate privately thought looked ludicrous. Because of his size and the arrogant

DR RYDER AND SON

way he treated them, the junior nurses called him Napoleon behind his back. Kate didn't; she felt that that kind of nickname could only interfere with the smooth running of the ward. But she had to admit that it fitted.

'Sister Storm? Entertaining friends?' It was spoken with a sneering smile and Kate took pleasure in answering.

'This is Dr Luke Ryder, a consultant oncologist from London. He's come to see Mike.'

Dr Norman's face altered rapidly. 'Dr Ryder, I'm Arthur Norman, junior doctor here. So pleased to see you.' A hand was thrust towards Luke so he had to take it. 'Dr Hamilton isn't here yet but I'd be pleased to show you round if you like.'

'I think I'd rather wait for Mike.'

As usual, Dr Norman didn't recognise the implied snub. He turned and said, 'If you've finished your coffee, Staff, I'm sure you've got work to do. I'll look after Dr Ryder.'

Pointedly she looked down at her half-empty cup, but she knew that the hint was futile. Then she glanced at Luke. She wondered what he thought of her ill-mannered dismissal, but he didn't appear to be about to say anything. Feeling vaguely annoyed, she said, 'I'll leave you both in my office then,' and swept out. Dr Luke Ryder might be useful in a fight but he didn't back up his friends. Not that he was a friend; she'd only just met him. So why did she feel so annoyed?

'Are you all right, Sister? Isn't he gorgeous?' Jenny came bustling past, pink-faced with excitement.

'Isn't who gorgeous?' asked Kate, knowing very well whom Jenny meant.

'That man there; what's his name? Is he a parent or something? I suppose he's a bit old for me.'

'That man there is Dr Luke Ryder, consultant oncologist. He's a very clever man, but I don't think he's gorgeous.'

The irrepressible Jenny giggled. 'Every time you lie,

Sister, you get a little black mark on your soul. Of course you think he's gorgeous.' She moved on too quickly to see the slight tinge of red on Kate's cheekbones.

As Kate pressed on with the never-ending work of the ward she found herself thinking about Dr Luke Ryder. She was irritated that he hadn't smiled at her once. Most men did, and Kate knew that she was attractive. He was probably married—though she'd noticed that there was no ring on his finger. Perhaps he had personal problems; perhaps he was. . . Kate realised that she'd been standing motionless in front of the drugs register for nearly five minutes. This was ridiculous; she'd probably never see the man again in her life.

In fact she saw him again that afternoon. Jamie Bartlett had to give a bone-marrow sample and have a lumbar puncture. Kate was called to assist and found that Luke was to look on as Mike and Dr Norman performed the two tiny operations.

'I gather you've met Luke,' Mike said genially as they walked to Jamie's room. 'I've been telling him how this ward wouldn't be half as efficient without you.'

'You just say that because I bribe you with chocolate biscuits,' she joked.

'I didn't get a chocolate biscuit,' Luke put in, straight-faced as always, but this time she felt that there might be just a touch of humour intended. It rather pleased her. What pleased her more was the sight of Dr Norman's disagreeable face. He obviously thought that any conversation should include him.

'I gather you're not a paediatric oncologist, Dr Ryder,' he said, carefully pushing his way between Kate and Luke. 'Do you feel there are many differences. . .?' Kate deliberately stopped listening. Behind the two men's backs Mike grinned and winked at her.

There was a small treatment room on the ward and so no need to take Jamie to theatre. Kate's first job was to reassure the little boy while a short-acting general anaesthetic was fed through the drip into his hand. When

22 **DR RYDER AND SON**

he was unconscious she helped to roll him onto his side and draw his knees up. Then she held him steady as the doctors inserted a needle between two of his vertebrae and collected a few drops of spinal fluid. Analysis would show whether the leukaemic cells had infiltrated the central nervous system.

The next task was to take a sample of bone marrow. Mike carefully fed a thicker needle into Jamie's hip-bone and drew off a small amount. For Kate it was routine. Not for Jamie. Examination of the sample would show if he was suffering from leukaemia and, if so, what sort.

Kate returned Jamie to his bed and reassured his anxious mother that everything had gone well. Then she went back to her office. Her day was nearly over and she found herself suffering from real fatigue. This was new, and she didn't like it.

The phone rang. It was Mrs Stock, half-tearful, half-angry. As much as she could Mrs Stock stayed in hospital with her daughter, but she had other children and had needed to take a day away.

'How could he do it?' Mrs Stock sobbed. 'He came back early off the rig and didn't come home first. No, he had a few drinks and then came to torment you. I've told him, Sister, that he's not to go near the hospital. He can go straight back to sea as far as I care. He's—'

Gently Kate managed to calm the lady down, told her that she understood and that Mr Stock would be welcome to see his daughter just so long as he obeyed the hospital rules. Finally, a much calmer Mrs Stock rang off. Kate sighed.

There was a knock and she shouted, 'Come in,' wondering what new problem there would be to plague her. But it wasn't a problem. Luke Ryder opened the door and she was amazed at the wave of exhilaration that swept through her.

'I have to go now,' he said. 'I just wanted to say thank you for letting me see round your ward.'

That was courteous, she thought. He didn't have to

GILL SANDERSON

say it at all. 'I hope it's proved useful,' she said. 'A pity you couldn't stay longer.'

He nodded gravely. 'I should have liked to. But I'm flying down to London tomorrow morning. A day's conference, and then back home.'

She didn't know why she said it. It just burst out. 'There's a ward party tonight in the nurses' home. Why don't you come along? We've booked the common room.'

For the first time he smiled, and his face was transformed. 'D'you know I think I will? I'd like that very much.'

'See you about half past eight, then?' she asked.

'About half past eight. Until then, good evening.'

She wondered why she so suddenly felt elated.

CHAPTER TWO

SISTER Denise Cowley's fortieth birthday was only an excuse. Aladdin Ward always had good parties. The doctors, nurses and ancillary staff were a tightly bonded team; occasionally they liked to relax together as well as work together. The work—treating children with cancer—was physically and emotionally demanding. Sometimes it was necessary to laugh and dance and talk halfway through the night to get away from the constant strain.

For a couple of hours Kate helped get things ready, cutting sandwiches and arranging tables, while others set up the disco and lined the walls with coloured twinkling lights. Then she obeyed the cheerful, shouted instructions and retired to her own room to change.

After a shower, with a towel knotted round her, she thoughtfully examined her wardrobe. Two dresses were taken out, held against her and returned to their hangers. Then she decided. Her black skirt, fitting tightly round her trim hips but flaring so she could dance. A good party skirt. With it she'd wear black stockings with seams. And for a top. . . She realised that she'd known all along what she was going to choose; the idea just took some getting used to. The white silk blouse she'd bought nine months ago but never yet dared to wear. Kate rummaged through her underwear drawer, looking for a pretty, lacy half-cup bra. Tonight she intended to look stunning!

She loved parties and for some reason she seemed to be looking forward to this one more than usual. Why? Kate was always ruthlessly honest with herself and the faintest of blushes touched her cheeks as she forced herself to confront the reason. She was hoping that Luke

24

Ryder would come to the party. He'd made an impression on her—not when he'd subdued Mr Stock or when she'd learned that he was an eminent oncologist, but the first time he'd smiled. Then he'd changed from a doctor into an incredibly attractive man.

She slipped off the towel and reached for her body lotion. He probably wouldn't come. And if he did he wouldn't want to talk to her. But he might, a little voice inside her said, and she sat to take extra care with her make-up.

The party had only just started when she got there but already the room was resounding to the thump of the disco and the little dance floor was nearly full. None of her friends believed in that rubbish about it being smart to arrive late.

'Who's looking wonderful tonight? Marry me, Kate, and we'll live on love and chocolate biscuits.'

Kate was kissed loudly on the cheek by Malcolm, a male nurse from Mother Goose Ward. There was barely time to swallow a glass of punch before she was swept onto the dance floor. She was a fluid, graceful dancer, and Malcolm had enough sense not to interfere with her. She gave herself to the music, holding Malcolm lightly and moving feet, hips and shoulders to the rhythm throbbing from the disco.

After a couple of tunes Malcolm smiled at her and said, 'Being with you almost convinces me that I can dance myself. Come on; I want another drink.' He led her courteously back to the edge of the room and offered to find her a seat.

'No, thanks, Malcolm; I want to meet people.' They parted amiably.

'Now, if this is a waltz or a quickstep then I shall ask you for the pleasure,' a voice behind her said, and she turned to smile at Mike Hamilton.

'I think it's one or the other,' she said demurely, 'but if you want I could ask the DJ to find us a veleta.'

DR RYDER AND SON

'Far too dangerous. If you will accompany me I will risk my old bones in whatever particular step this music demands.' He looked mournfully at the gyrating figures around them. 'It *looks* like a cannibal war dance.'

Not altogether to Kate's surprise, Mike turned out to be a more than adequate partner. He had far more sense of rhythm than Malcolm.

It was a good party. She wandered round the room, chatting to friends and colleagues, being introduced to their new boyfriends and girlfriends. When she offered to help further with the little buffet, her friend Denise Cowley told her to go and enjoy herself, that she'd done quite enough already. Kate remembered Mike's request and arranged with Denise to do her Friday shift.

'It suits me really well,' Denise said. 'Bob wanted to take me to dinner for my birthday.' She looked at Kate sympathetically. 'You know, Kate, if you constantly do favours for people there comes a time when you're taken for granted. Don't you ever think of anything but work?'

'It's my life and I love it,' Kate said lightly. 'Have a good evening out with Bob.' But as she walked back into the main room she wondered if Denise was right. Perhaps there should be something more to her life than work. She felt a sudden unexpected pang of loneliness. It would be nice to have someone to love, and be loved by.

However, her moment of doubt soon passed. There were friends whom she hadn't seen for a week or two and even more hospital gossip. One by one the staff actually on duty on Aladdin Ward slipped down in uniform to congratulate Denise and have a swift, non-alcoholic drink.

Kate danced again. Having found out what actually went into the innocent-tasting punch, she decided to stick to white wine in future. She was pleased that she'd decided to wear the white blouse. A couple of her female friends said how much it suited her. Actually, Jenny Metcalfe said, 'You *do* look sexy, Sister.' When Kate told her that eighteen-year-olds looked sexy, twenty-

GILL SANDERSON 27

five-year-olds looked smart, Jenny just grinned and said, 'Nuts.'

None of her male friends commented but it was obvious what they thought, and she experienced a tiny shiver of feminine naughtiness when she felt them looking at her.

She was enjoying herself; it was a good party. The room was hotting up so she went to the tiny bar to get a long glass of iced mineral water. Then out of the shadows in the corridor a tall figure moved decisively towards her and her heart lurched. She realised that, for her, the party hadn't yet really begun.

Luke Ryder had accepted her invitation. Like all the other men he was dressed casually, in dark trousers and a blue denim shirt, open at the neck. His face was serious as he said, 'Good evening, Sister Storm.'

She shook her head and said, 'I'm not Sister Storm; tonight I'm Kate. You're not Dr Ryder either; tonight you're Luke until the party's over.'

'And tomorrow?' he queried.

'Tomorrow we change back to our working selves again. You can be Doctor if you want, and I'll be Sister.'

'Can you do that? I mean change roles so easily?'

She smiled, a little breathlessly. 'I can do it. I'm sure you can if you try.'

'Then I'll certainly try. Tonight will be a little holiday from normal life—no questions, no duties, no responsibilities. Tomorrow we can forget it ever happened.'

'This is a party, Luke; it should leave happy memories. And any act may have consequences.'

'That is true,' he said slowly.

Since he seemed disinclined to move, she reached forward and took his hand. 'Come on in. I'll get you a drink first, then we can go and meet people.'

For the first time his stern features relaxed and he smiled. 'If there's any beer I'd love one, Kate. But I didn't come here to meet people. If it's possible I'd like to sit and just talk to you.'

28 **DR RYDER AND SON**

'The bar's this way,' she croaked. Things were moving far too quickly for her.

The bar was in an alcove in the corridor and it was Malcolm's turn to serve. When she asked him for a beer he took a plastic mug from a pile. Then he glanced at Luke and reached under the counter to find a glass. When he was sure that Luke wasn't looking he winked conspiratorially at Kate. She sighed. The trouble with friends was that they took a keen interest in your affairs.

She could feel it as, glasses in hand, she and Luke stepped into the main room. In spite of the beat of the disco there was a subdued hum of comment as people noticed them. One or two, of course, had already met Luke that afternoon. The rest had not, and there was the usual quest for information. Kate heard the irrepressible Jenny Metcalfe whispering to her friends, 'I told you he was gorgeous and he is, isn't he? Kate didn't tell us she'd invited him.'

Kate realised that she would have to face some kind of inquisition the next day. 'Let's go and say hello to Mike,' she said, hurrying Luke away before Jenny said anything else. 'I know he'll be pleased to see you.'

'That will be nice.'

She led the way to Mike's table.

Mike looked both delighted and surprised. 'Come to a party, Luke? I didn't think this was your kind of thing at all. Had I known I would have invited you myself.'

'Somebody rather special got me here.' Luke turned to study her gravely. 'I envy you your ward sister, Mike.'

'I've got a good staff all round,' Mike said loyally.

Kate didn't know what to feel. She had the panicky sense of being thrown into a situation beyond her control. For a moment she was content to sit at the table and listen to the two men chat.

Then the music softened and she heard the DJ shout, 'Enough of this acrobatic-style dancing. You'll all wear yourselves out and the night is still young. We'll have a change of mood. For all you young lovers, here's something slow and sweet, so get up and smoo-oo-ooch!'

Luke turned and held out his hand. 'There's an attractive invitation,' he said. 'Would you like to get up and smooch?'

She felt unable to reply, but took his hand and let him lead her onto the floor.

She didn't recognise the music but she reacted to it instantly. Strings and woodwind played gently together, suggesting distant, sun-kissed beaches and warm, tropical nights. Around them couples swayed languorously together, arms wrapped loosely about each other.

He pulled her gently towards him and clasped her round the waist. She rested her hands on his upper arms, feeling the curve of muscles beneath. They began to dance, responding to the subtlety of the beat.

He used all his body to guide her, urging her to move by the most delicate of pressures on her thighs and waist. To her great joy she discovered that he was a marvellous dancer, with an instinctive feeling for mood and rhythm. Contentedly she gave herself to the music and his guidance. As he bowed his head towards hers she closed her eyes.

Perhaps it was a mistake. Without sight her other senses were enhanced. She was intensely conscious of the warmth of his body, of the distant muskiness of his cologne, of the tiniest of raspings as his chin touched her forehead. He held her so closely that her breasts pressed against his chest, and through the silk of her blouse and the lace of her bra she felt her nipples grow, swelling to twin aroused peaks. He'll notice, she thought in panic; her eyes flicked open and she pushed him away. He had noticed. He smiled down at her, then inexorably pulled her closer again. Sighing, she complied. There appeared to be nothing she could do.

To her the dance seemed to last for ever, but it couldn't have been longer than four or five minutes. Then the music ended, there was a loud fanfare and all the lights

30 DR RYDER AND SON

of the room went on. Kate stepped back from her partner and stared at him, as if in incredulity that their idyll could be broken. He stared back equally sadly, then took her hand and led her back to Mike's table.

'And now, ladies and gentlemen,' shouted the DJ, 'the main purpose of the evening. Let's hear it for Denise, the birthday girl!'

To applause from all, Denise was half escorted, half pushed into the middle of the dance floor. Then all the lights went out again and to a great cheer a cake with forty burning candles was carried forward. With a huge puff Denise managed to blow them all out. The lights went on again as everyone sang, 'Happy birthday to you.'

'She's obviously very popular,' Luke commented.

Kate nodded. 'She's a good ward sister. We're a tightly knit team; we celebrate everyone's birthday.'

He nodded slowly. 'Everyone's obviously enjoying themselves. And yet in the next couple of days all of you will be working with children—knowing full well that some of those children will die.'

It struck Kate like a blow. It was true, of course, but tonight was for celebration. It was not the time for such dark thoughts. She felt surprised that Luke should have had to say such a thing; he must be in charge of patients whose prognosis was much worse than those of the children in Aladdin Ward. She tried to explain.

'It's as if you have two lives. When you're on the ward you have to feel for your charges. You'd be no good as a nurse if you didn't. If one dies then we all weep. But you can't drag all that misery into your life off the ward. Then you've got to switch off completely and enjoy yourself.'

'And you can do that? Switch off completely?'

'I have to. But there are times when I feel a very old twenty-five-year-old.'

Mike had walked to the centre of the floor. He made a short speech saying what a fine nurse Denise was,

GILL SANDERSON

then, to applause from all, kissed her and waved for her present to be brought on. It was a dinner service; over the past few weeks her staff had carefully discovered the pattern she liked best. Tears ran down Denise's cheeks as she thanked everyone. Then the music started up again and the floor began to fill with dancers.

'Early night for me, I think,' Mike said. 'Luke, I'll be in touch in a day or two.' He reached out to shake Luke's hand.

'I'll walk you to your car,' Luke said. 'It's getting warm in here, anyhow. Kate, would you like a breath of fresh air?'

'I'd love one,' she said.

Luke and Kate stood on the edge of the car park and watched Mike's old green Daimler as its lights flicked on and it purred slowly forward. There was a last friendly wave from the driver's window. She shivered, not because she was cold but because they were alone. The odd light in the dark nurses' home behind them, the distant strain of the disco only seemed to emphasise their solitude.

He put his arm round her. 'Do you want to go straight back or would you like to walk for a while?'

It was only April but it was balmy—quite warm enough to walk in the night air. 'There's a sunken garden that way,' she said. 'We could sit there for a while.' Hesitantly she put her arm round his waist. Then she removed it.

'I don't know you very well,' she said. 'I don't even know that you're not married.'

He chuckled, reached behind him for her arm and replaced it round him. 'Would it matter? Couldn't you do what you do with your work? Just switch off and forget about it till tomorrow?'

'No, I could not,' she said firmly. 'You know very well that that's something quite different. Now, are you married or not?'

There was a moment's silence. She could feel her

palms dampen, her heart pound in her chest. Then he said, 'I'm not married. I was once but I'm now firmly and properly and legally divorced. And if you're interested I was not what is quaintly called the guilty party.'

She had no difficulty believing him; the bitterness in his voice was evident. 'I'm sorry,' she said softly. 'I didn't mean to pry.'

'Not your fault, Kate. You've every right to ask.'

She led him so that they stepped down into the sunken garden. On each side of them were banks of shrubs and flowers; white sprays gleamed faintly in the starlight.

He stopped and turned towards her. His face and his body were in shadow but she could feel his presence as clearly as if it were day. Gently he pulled her towards him so that their bodies were touching, as closely as they had been in their one dance. 'I don't know you very well,' she said tremulously.

'How long does it take?' His arms wrapped round her, tightened, and he stooped his head towards hers.

First he kissed her on the forehead, his lips warm and slightly damp. Then he feathered kisses down the angle of her eye and jaw, touching her with the delicacy of a butterfly.

Kate sighed, a great breath of anticipation, and tilted her head backwards so that her face was raised to his. She had been kissed by men in the dark before, but none of them had ever made her pulses race as this man did. He was gentle, as if knowing that there was nothing she could do to resist.

When finally his lips met hers they were tentative, delicate, as if he was giving her one last chance to change her mind. This she didn't want. She curved her arm round his neck and pulled him down to her, pressing her body against his. His own arms tightened. She moaned softly, her mouth opening as his tongue caressed the sensitive skin inside her lips. For an eternal moment she felt as if they were fused into one, tied by the sweetness of a kiss.

GILL SANDERSON 33

Then he broke away. His ragged breathing told her what his emotions were, and under the warmth of his chest she could feel the rapid beating of his heart.

'Kate,' he muttered, 'things are going too fast. I think we should go back.'

'But I don't want to,' she protested plaintively.

'D'you think I do? This has never happened before. I. . .I think we should. . . I didn't intend. . .'

'I didn't intend either,' she said.

For a moment longer they stayed pressed together, then with infinite reluctance he took his arms from around her. 'Cancer wards,' he said. 'The staff work hard and play hard.'

'We're not on the ward now. And I didn't think you were playing then,' she said.

'No, I wasn't playing. Now let's get back to the party.'

She let him take her hand and lead her back towards the distant music. Her feelings were in turmoil; she just couldn't understand what had happened to her. Of one thing she was certain. She'd never felt like this before.

One or two people looked at them a little curiously as they re-entered the party, but none of her friends was so impolite as to ask where they'd been. She couldn't understand it; couldn't everyone detect the change in her? Wasn't it obvious that her entire life had changed? When she glanced at Luke she could see no change in *him*; he seemed to have reassumed the faintly distant air of the hospital consultant.

'Would you like another drink?' he asked. Showing a chink of human feeling, he went on, 'I could certainly do with one myself.'

'I think I'd like a whisky.' Normally she would never drink spirits at a party but this evening hadn't been normal. He said nothing but looked at her assessingly. Then he asked Malcolm for the drink and had another beer himself.

The party was now entering the boisterous stage but they had no difficulty in finding a table in a dark corner

34 DR RYDER AND SON

where they could sit and talk uninterrupted. Kate took a healthy swig at the large whisky and promptly burst into a bout of coughing. He didn't laugh at her but slapped her gently on the back. The touch of his hand on her bare skin was still electric.

'We've only just met,' he said. 'I kissed you once and I could feel the passion in you. I wondered what I'd done.'

'I know. But you felt the same for me, didn't you?' She was glad but not surprised that he didn't attempt to deny it.

'I think you may be the most exciting woman I've ever met. But I've learned that emotion is not always a good guide in life.' He sipped his beer and then said, 'Earlier you said that you had two lives. You could feel for ill children on the ward but when you left you could switch off. Can you switch off me?'

'Certainly I can if I want to,' she said. Her entire being screamed that that was a lie, but her face remained open and frank.

'I wouldn't want you—'

'Dr Ryder, here you are. I've been looking for you. I heard you were at the party so I thought I'd drop in for a chat.'

Kate looked up and felt like groaning. Looming over them, glass in hand, was Dr Norman. There were only two chairs at the table but that didn't stop him. He pushed his empty glass towards Kate and said, 'I think I'll have another brandy. Fetch me a drink, Sister, would you?'

'No,' said Kate.

Dr Norman blinked, as if unable to understand. 'But I'm—'

'The bar's over there,' she snapped, 'and you're interrupting our conversation. Good evening, Dr Norman.' She turned her head back to Luke, who was witnessing the scene with a half-smile.

For a moment Dr Norman stood there obviously with

no idea what to do next. Then he muttered something and swiftly walked away.

Luke said, 'You never stop amazing me. You have such a gorgeous, guileless face that everyone thinks you must have a sweet nature to match. And yet underneath you can be as hard as steel.'

'I don't need to be as hard as steel to deal with him,' she grumbled. 'And I've just done the wrong thing. It makes for a quieter life to keep him happy.' Then she asked, '*Do* you think I have a gorgeous face?'

'You're fishing.' He smiled. 'You're—' They were interrupted again.

This time it was Malcolm, with a serious expression on his face. 'Dr Ryder, isn't it?' he asked. 'A lady's just been on the phone; she said it was important. This is her name and number.' He handed Luke a slip of paper. 'Will you ring her straight back, please? You can use the phone behind the bar.'

With a muttered 'Excuse me' Luke stood and headed for the bar. Malcolm looked at Kate and shrugged. 'A doctor's life is a busy one,' she said.

Two minutes later Luke was back. Even in the dim light she could tell the difference in him. His eyes were distant; there was a remoteness in his very bearing. 'Something personal has cropped up,' he said. 'I have to leave. It's been an enjoyable evening, Kate, but good-night. I'm sure we'll meet again.' Then he was gone.

She took a sip of her whisky and gasped as the fiery liquid seared down her throat. A shadow fell across her table and she looked up to see Dr Norman—again. Unpleasantly he said, 'Now your boyfriend's gone you might as well dance with me.'

'Get lost,' she snarled, with such venom that he stumbled away. This is a night to remember, she thought; what is happening to me? I've never in my life spoken to anyone like that.

Her next visitor was more welcome. Jenny Metcalfe tripped across, bubbling and excited. Sitting down, she

DR RYDER AND SON

explained that she just *had* to tell somebody, it was all very exciting.

'Of course, I've seen him before on the ward but he's never said anything to me and he must be at least twenty-one. But he says that he's always been too shy to talk to me and would I like to go to the jazz club next Wednesday night with a group of them. What d'you think I should wear?'

Jenny had fallen for Allan Fordyce, one of the male nurses. Kate wasn't expected to comment but just to listen—which she was happy to do. After a while the shy Allan came over to the table, blushed, said good evening and escorted Jenny away.

How simple it must be to be eighteen, Kate thought from her vast age of twenty-five. Suddenly she felt very old. The now noisy party around her didn't excite her as it once would have done and she thought that she might as well go back to her room.

She called goodnight to one or two of her closer friends and made for the exit. In the deserted corridor there was a mirror and she stopped to examine her appearance. Gloomily she wondered why she'd bothered to put on her daring new blouse. She knew that she looked attractive in it, but the man she'd wanted to attract had been summoned away by some female or other.

She heard steps coming down the corridor. Then there was a blast of alcoholic breath and the drunken voice of Dr Norman said, 'My favourite nurse. At last I've got her alone.'

She just couldn't believe what happened next. He stood close behind her, put an arm over her shoulder and forced his hand down the open front of her blouse, right inside her bra. His roughness tore off a tiny pearl button and for a frozen second she watched it spiralling to the floor.

Suddenly all her anger boiled over. She forgot that she was Sister Storm, known for her patience and skill in dealing with troublesome or irate visitors. She'd had enough. First she dragged his hand upwards. Then she whirled round and slapped him across the face, with all the power gained through hours playing squash. The noise of the slap echoed along the corridor.

Things seemed to happen in slow motion. There was Dr Norman's reddened face, his expression turning to disbelief as her hand crashed into him. He lurched backwards, lost his balance, put out a hand to save himself. His head hit the wall.

'Next time you do that to me,' Kate spat, 'I'll break your neck.'

Then, being a nurse, she knelt down to attend to him.

CHAPTER THREE

IT WAS work as usual next morning. As Kate walked over to the ward she hoped that her friends and colleagues there would carry on as if nothing had happened, as if the loudly complaining Dr Norman had not been carted off to Casualty. In fact this was what they did, and perversely she then wanted them to say something— an expression of sympathy or solidarity, a joke— anything would do. Instead they carried on with the unremitting toil.

First, of course, there was the report from the night staff nurse. No new admissions, no great change in anyone's condition. Nevertheless, they went through the ward name by name. Then Kate took the key to the drug trolley and spent half an hour on the medicine round. By now she knew all the dosages, but she still double-checked in the drug card index on the trolley. This also gave her a chance to look in on everyone.

Halfway through the morning Kate saw Jenny hurry away from the ward and make for the staff toilet. Just before opening the door she pulled a tissue from her pocket and dabbed at her eyes. Kate sighed. She knew what Jenny was going through.

Tapping on the toilet door, she called, 'Jenny, I know what's wrong. You can come and cry in my office and we'll have a coffee afterwards.' After a pause she said, 'There's no shame in crying. We all do sometimes.'

The door opened, revealing Jenny's tear-streaked face. Compassionately Kate put her arm round her shoulders. 'It's Perry Harrison, isn't it?' she asked quietly.

Jenny nodded. 'He's dying,' she sobbed. 'Dr Doyle says he won't last the day. His mum and dad are sitting

38

GILL SANDERSON 39

with him, holding his hands and waiting for him to die, and he's only ten.'

'Come and sit down. I'll see you're not disturbed for a few minutes and then we'll have a chat.'

Jenny looked alarmed. 'But I'm behind in my work. I've got to help with—'

Kate cut her off. 'There's time for you to sit quietly for a quarter of an hour. The work will wait.'

She ushered Jenny into her office then went to ask Fiona Hastie, a more experienced nurse, to cover Jenny's work. 'It's her first death on here, isn't it?' Fiona asked. 'Poor kid. You never get used to it, but the first is always the worst. Don't worry; I can cope with the next hour.'

Next Kate looked in on the little room where Perry Harrison was lying. His parents had been told some time ago that there was no hope of their son recovering and had had counselling. Now it was just a matter of time, and that time was running out.

Kate went back to her office and arranged for Mike to be called. Even though he'd spoken to the parents before, he felt that he should always be available when the child died. Then she turned to Jenny, who was sitting, silent, head bowed, in the corner.

In a matter-of-fact tone Kate said, 'You know the figures but I'm just going to remind you. First of all, Perry's in no pain. We gave him morphine and he'll quietly slip away without ever regaining consciousness. The only people who are suffering are his parents—and the staff who've cared for Perry. And the parents now look to the staff for support.'

Jenny made no reply to this. Kate poured her a coffee and added two spoonfuls of sugar. Briefly she remembered how Luke had done the same for her yesterday. No time to think of him now!

She went on, 'The next thing to remember is how well we now do. Eighty per cent of children with acute lymphoblastic leukaemia now attain complete

40 DR RYDER AND SON

remission. Twenty years ago eighty per cent of children died.'

'Children still die. And I'll never get used to it.'

'You mustn't ever get used to it. You'll be no good as a nurse if you can't feel for your patients. What you must do is both feel sympathy and distance yourself. It's hard but it can be done. If you don't switch off when you leave the ward then you'll never survive.'

At long last Jenny's head came up. Defiantly she said, 'I'm going to survive. I want to.'

'I hope you do. Because I believe you've got the makings of a first-class nurse in one of the hardest specialities there is.'

She waited a while as Jenny sipped her coffee and then said formally, 'When you've finished your coffee, Nurse Metcalfe, you can go to help Nurse Hastie.'

'Yes, Sister. I'll be right there.'

Kate hid her weary smile. Nurse Metcalfe would be all right now. She only wished that she could give herself some of the confidence she'd just instilled in Jenny.

The bane of Kate's life was the paperwork. She knew it was necessary, she wouldn't have wanted anyone else to do it, but there seemed such a lot of it. She was a nurse not a clerk! When Mike tapped at her door and asked for a drink and ten minutes of her time she put down her pen with relish.

Mike accepted his coffee and his biscuits and sat in the easy chair with a sigh. 'Just had a word with your student nurse,' he said. 'Young Jenny. She'll be a good nurse in time, Kate. You're teaching her well.'

Kate lifted her shoulders in embarrassment. 'She just needed someone to listen to her.'

'Hmm. I wish it was as easy as that.' He bit into his biscuit and then looked up with a grin. 'I've just been hospital visiting,' he said. 'A patient referred from Casualty last night and kept in overnight for observation because of an injury to his head.' He beamed. 'Perhaps it's not surprising how many drunks manage to hurt themselves.'

She blushed. 'Mike, I want to explain——'

He cut her off. 'There's nothing to explain. I've worked with the pair of you; I could tell what happened just by knowing both your characters. Incidentally, one of the nurses on the ward asked if you could be given a medal for services to the nursing profession.'

'I don't really want that kind of talk,' she said. 'It's unprofessional.'

'True. But it does reflect something.' He went on, 'Dr Norman told me he'll be back at work in a couple of days. He did mention that he was contemplating some kind of official complaint. I had to tell him that he would get neither sympathy nor support and that any such complaint would be professional suicide. After some thought he found he agreed with me.'

'Did you do that for me?' she asked curiously.

He shook his head. 'No, Kate. I did it for my patients and those who look after them.' Then he peered at her over his half-moon glasses and said, 'Well, perhaps a little bit for you.'

She looked at him thoughtfully. He looked benign— everybody's favourite uncle. But she knew that in what he thought were the best interests of his patients he could be quite unscrupulous and utterly ruthless. 'Well, thank you,' she said.

'Dr Norman will be with us for another two months. Then he'll leave this ward, and, I suspect, this hospital. Now that's him finished with. I want to talk about you.'

She felt apprehensive again. Yesterday Mike had not finished what he'd had to say; apparently he was going to now. 'What about me?' she asked.

'Tomorrow's Friday. You're coming in to help me deal with the Vincent family. On Saturday I've arranged with the chief nursing officer for you to take three weeks' holiday.'

42   DR RYDER AND SON

Her amazement and anger were total. 'You've done what?'

Imperturbably he said, 'You had no other plans, did you?'

'I'm quite capable of organising my own holidays, if I want to. And I have a ward to run.'

'Other people can run the ward nearly as well as you. But if you carry on as you are doing they'll be running it an awful lot better.'

Kate felt molten fury at this betrayal. 'How dare you?'

'I dare, Kate, because I'm your friend, and because I'm concerned about the welfare of our patients and the smooth running of this ward. I'm a doctor. And you are suffering from exhaustion. You *must* have a change.'

There was silence as she grappled with the unwelcome ideas that Mike had provoked. Her first reaction was to tell him that he was being ridiculous. Then her native honesty took over and she conceded that he might have a point. There had been times recently when she'd felt lethargic, uninterested. After that, realisation came in full. She did need a change.

'All right, Mike,' she said quietly. 'I'll get away somewhere for a while. Perhaps I have been overdoing it.' Troubled, she thought over the past few weeks. 'I've not made any really big mistakes, have I?'

'You've made no mistakes at all,' he reassured her. 'Perhaps you just lost that fine edge.'

She knew what he meant but she didn't want to discuss it. Trying to change the subject, she said, 'When you'd gone last night I had a long chat with Luke. He's quite different when you get to know him—not as stiff.' She wondered if her casual remark betrayed how she really felt, but Mike didn't seem to notice anything.

'He's a good doctor,' he said. 'And his private life recently has been truly dreadful. I just don't know how he's coped. However. . .tomorrow Sally Vincent is coming in. I'll be here, of course, but I'd like you to. . .'

Calmly Kate discussed the arrangements that would

have to be made. Mike's hints about Luke's life had only teased her. She wanted to know more—but couldn't think of any way to ask.

Predictably the next day was hectic. Sally Vincent, as always, was an ideal patient. Sally's family were tearful, hysterical, demanding. Kate knew that their concern only came from love, but it was trying all the same. She was a medical nurse, not a social worker! The moment she thought this she felt guilty. As she never tired of telling her junior nurses, they treated the family, not just the patient.

She was glad when the morning was nearly finished. She realised just how right Mike had been. She did need a break.

'Have you decided where you're going to go yet?' Mike asked when they managed to snatch a quiet five minutes in the afternoon.

She shook her head. 'Now it's arranged I'm really looking forward to a break. But I couldn't work up enough enthusiasm last night to book somewhere. And there's no one I could go with at such short notice.'

'Do you mind if I interfere with your life again? I've got a suggestion.'

'Suggest away,' she said cheerfully.

From inside his white coat Mike took a piece of paper and handed it to her. 'There's a new paediatric wing just opened at that hospital near York—they call it the Wolds and Dales. I know Marion Pitts, the consultant there, quite well. She phoned me for a chat last night. Why don't you drive over tomorrow and see her? I think she could have something for you.'

'What sort of something?'

Mike shrugged. 'It's a kind of job, but not half as intensive as the work you've been doing. You could get some country air, plenty of sleep, recharge your

DR RYDER AND SON

batteries. You wouldn't have to do any organising either. No messing with bookings and so on.'

That was a definite plus. She'd accepted that she needed a change, but finding one in her present listless state was difficult. Still. . .

'It all seems a bit odd,' Kate said suspiciously. 'Tell me a bit more.'

'I'd rather you went to find out for yourself.' He beamed. 'Now, have I ever let you down before?'

'Well, no,' she said. But then she remembered his well-deserved reputation for getting his own way, and wondered.

Next morning she woke rather looking forward to her change. It only took her half an hour to pack and then she was driving out of Manchester and onto the motorway leading over the Pennines. She was dressed in trousers and a scarlet sweater; for once she felt like being colourful.

When her father had died she'd had to sell their little house. After the debts had been paid there'd been just enough money left for one extravagance—and her new red car had been it. Unfortunately, she didn't seem to get much chance to use it.

Now, as the spring sun flashed on the grey-green hills of the Pennines rolling on each side of her, she wondered if too much of her time was spent in the hospital. There had to be something more to life. She had to get out more.

Perhaps inevitably her thoughts turned to the events of the past week. Had it really been necessary to hit Dr Norman so hard? She had to admit that her anger had been the result of frustrations that hadn't been entirely his fault. Then after a moment's reflection she decided that she wasn't in the least sorry. He'd deserved it.

What about Luke Ryder? She felt apprehensive even thinking about him. She was disappointed that he hadn't phoned her. He'd created a depth of feeling in her that was unsettling in its intensity. No man had ever had such

GILL SANDERSON 45

an instant effect on her. Perhaps she was more than usually vulnerable at the moment; that's why she needed a change. But she knew that when she felt more able to deal with her feelings she'd have to decide what to do about the man.

Near the top of the Pennines she stopped for a coffee and took in great breaths of the chilly mountain air. Then she checked her atlas for the fastest road to York. The sheer pleasure of travel gripped her. Perhaps her life was moving—not away from something but towards something.

Her tentative appointment with Dr Pitts was for late in the afternoon so there was plenty of time. She'd never visited York before and decided to stop in one of the park and ride sites. As she wandered round the centre, admiring the Minster, looking in the shops in the Shambles, she felt her spirits lightening. For a guilt-free hour she browsed round a bookshop and then bought herself a novel that she'd been promising herself to read for two years.

Then it was back to her car and onto the broad bypass that led to the east coast.

She liked the Wolds and Dales at once. Her own much loved hospital was built of smoke-grimed, late-Victorian brick, surrounded by little streets and factories. This hospital seemed like a village; there were trees, birds, shrubs and a distant view of hills. There was also plenty of parking space. She'd like to work here.

As directed, she found her way to Sparrow Ward and reported to the sister. There had obviously just been a ward round; the sister was carefully copying out the nursing directions from the large ward diary into the nursing card index. At Kate's request she bleeped Dr Pitts. This was an attractive, well-run ward—Kate noticed the space there was for everything and felt a little envious. Then a tall, raven-haired woman strode up and introduced herself as Dr Pitts. 'But I hope you'll call me Marion. Everyone does.'

'Well, I'm known as Kate,' Kate said, and followed as Marion led her down a corridor.

'How's Mike?' Marion asked as they walked purposefully onwards. 'I started paediatric oncology with him, you know. If I just learn half of what he knows I'll be happy.'

'He's well,' Kate said, 'and sends you his regards.'

Marion stopped outside a door and smiled. 'Is he just the same? Looks like Father Christmas in plain clothes, but underneath he's a cunning old devil who'll bend any rule if he thinks it will benefit his patients?'

'Dr Hamilton is a senior consultant at our hospital,' Kate answered drily. 'And I'm afraid that's a perfect description of him.'

Marion giggled. Then her face turned serious and she waved for Kate to look through the window in the door, into a tiny side-ward. 'This is Sean, aged nine,' she said. 'Acute lymphoblastic leukaemia. Two years ago he had his first course of chemotherapy. Unfortunately he then had a relapse. He's had a second course of chemotherapy so he's back in remission now and probably going home tomorrow.'

Kate peered in at a small boy in blue pyjamas. He was awake; she could see that his eyes were open. They looked unusually large under the scalp that was now nearly bald. He was lying on his bed, gazing at the ceiling. She guessed that that was all he had strength for. She felt a great rush of pity. A relapse after an initial course of chemotherapy wasn't good news.

'Will you be giving him a bone-marrow transplant?' she asked.

'It's the obvious thing to do,' Marion sighed. 'Unfortunately we can't get a match. Things are worse because he's got an unusually high white cell count. He's an only child; there are no brothers or sisters to be donors. We've tested his parents, of course, but we didn't really

GILL SANDERSON 47

expect a result. All we can do now is ask the computer to throw something up—and wait and hope.'

Kate nodded. She knew that if there was no one suitable in the immediate family finding a donor was almost impossible. It had been done—but it was uncommon.

'Is there any special reason why we're looking at Sean?' she asked.

'He's going home tomorrow. He's very weak and there's some risk of infection. Every two days he'll need a blood test, but really he doesn't need full-time medical attention.' Marion frowned. 'At present he's living with his grandmother. She's tough and intelligent, and life in her country house would be ideal for young Sean. But I would feel—well, more secure if there was a qualified medical person nearby.'

She turned to smile at Kate. 'Yesterday I phoned Mike and mentioned this case. He said he might have a solution. A nurse he knew could do with three weeks of country air. So, Kate, do you fancy the job?'

It came as rather a shock. But then as she considered the proposition she realised that there was a lot to be said for it. 'You'd only want me for three weeks?' she asked.

Marion nodded. 'After three weeks Sean should have made enough progress to be safely left with his grandmother. He should be much stronger. And, of course, the grandmother would be used to looking after him by then.'

Kate thought a little more. 'Perhaps I could spend a while with him,' she temporised, 'to see if we get on.'

'That's a good idea. Let me get you a coat.'

Two minutes later she was sitting beside the bed. Sean must have known that she'd entered the room but his gaze remained firmly fixed on the ceiling.

'Hello, Sean, I'm Kate Storm. Won't you be glad to go home tomorrow?'

The head slowly turned sideways. She almost gasped at the deep dark blue of his eyes.

'It will be very pleasant to go back to the country,'

48   DR RYDER AND SON

he said. 'Though my grandmother has visited me most days.' He spoke slowly and formally, as if each word had to be weighed. Kate knew that at this late stage of treatment even speaking would take a physical effort.

'I'd like to see your house,' she said. 'Perhaps I could come and stay with you.'

Those gorgeous eyes stared at her unblinkingly. Then he said, 'I think I'd like that. Someone. . .a bit nearer my age.'

She knew then that she'd take the job if she could. There was something attractive about the dignity of this child. He seemed older than he was. A thought flashed, unwelcome, through her mind: Knowing you might die makes you grow up fast.

For another five minutes she stayed and chatted. She did most of the talking—apart from anything else she didn't want to overtire the child. But she felt that he grew interested in her and responded to her presence.

When Marion waved to her from outside the ward she told Sean that she hoped to see him again soon. Then she slipped outside and said, 'He's a lovely child. If the job's available, I'll take it.'

Marion looked approving. 'Good. Now there's just a quick interview—I'm sure it will be a formality—and then we'll have a coffee and make final arrangements.'

Kate had thought that Marion was completely in charge—but she was willing to answer any further questions. They walked along gaily decorated corridors hung with pictures until they reached a quieter, carpeted area, obviously the offices of the senior members of the hospital. Marion tapped on a door, opened it, called, 'Sister Storm for you,' and ushered Kate inside.

It was quite a large room. At one end was a great picture window, giving a view of a rockery just outside then a panorama of cultivated fields rising to hills in the distance. There were the usual filing cabinets and office furniture in a pleasing light wood. There were also plants and flowers, and paintings and photographs on the walls,

GILL SANDERSON   **49**

showing that someone had an eye for line and colour.

A man stood up behind the desk. Against the window behind him he was just a dark silhouette. 'How nice to see you, Sister Storm,' he said.

The voice was so familiar that she recognised it at once. But the shock at hearing it was so great that for a moment she was speechless. Finally a word reached her dry lips. 'Luke!' she said. It sounded like an accusation.

'Dr Ryder,' he returned. 'Do have a seat.'

Three days before she had met two men in one body. There had been the saturnine professional doctor and then the lover who had moved her as had no other man. Now she was facing the doctor again and she wasn't sure she liked it. This wasn't right. She felt an angry suspicion growing inside her. She'd been manipulated.

Somehow she managed to sit in the chair he indicated. She forced herself to be calm, to act as if they were only acquaintances. A thought struck her with a pain that was almost physical. Perhaps to him they were only casual acquaintances.

He sat himself and unsmilingly said, 'The last time we met you said you could change roles easily. We're not Kate and Luke now. Now we're Dr Ryder and Sister Storm.'

She couldn't help herself. 'Dr Ryder and Sister Storm? It sounds like the name of a country-and-western folk group.'

The smallest of reluctant smiles touched his lips. 'It has a certain—resonance,' he admitted. 'I just wished to point out that this was a purely professional meeting.'

'Of course.' She took a deep breath. 'I'm a little surprised to see you here; I thought after London you'd want to work in another big city.'

'Why?' He turned and waved a hand at the scene outside. 'Which would you prefer—London or countryside like this? I've got a little cottage in the village over there and I can walk here in ten minutes.'

'It must be nice,' she agreed, then frowned. She was

50

DR RYDER AND SON

getting over her shock now; she didn't want to indulge in pointless social chat. 'Did you have any part in the trickery that got me here?' she demanded angrily.

He remained calm. 'There was no trickery,' he said. 'Marion phoned Mike Hamilton about some matter and explained she was looking for a nurse. Mike then suggested your name. Marion did ask me and I told her that I'd only met you briefly but that I thought you'd be an excellent nurse.'

'Did you tell her that we'd met socially as well as professionally?'

For a moment she thought that she saw him flinch; that barb had hurt. However, he merely said, 'This is a professional matter.'

'In that case you'd better interview me to assess my professional competence,' she said, not caring if the tightness of her words revealed the seething anger within.

'That might be a good idea. Although your references are excellent.' He paused for a moment and then said silkily, 'But sending a colleague to Casualty isn't much of a recommendation, is it, Sister?'

The question was so unexpected that she didn't know whether to laugh or lose her temper properly. In the end she defiantly said, 'No, it's not. I'm sorry he hurt his head. But under similar circumstances I would act in exactly the same way again.'

'Hmm.' He looked at her shrewdly. 'Do you feel that your work has been getting a bit too stressful lately? I ask this because Mike said you hadn't had a holiday for quite a while.'

'Are you an expert on stress, Doctor?' she asked bitingly.

He didn't respond in kind. 'I think all doctors who deal with cancer have to deal with stress,' he said. 'As, of course, do all nurses.' His voice was gentle, thoughtful, and she felt a little ashamed.

After a moment she answered, 'I must be honest. It's

GILL SANDERSON

51

possible that. . .well, I've been overdoing it just a bit.'

'It's an easy trap to fall into.' He brooded for a moment and then went on, 'When we last met you told me that a good nurse could sympathise on the ward and yet switch off all feelings when she left.'

'It's the only way to survive,' Kate said. 'I'm sure you know that very well.'

'I do. But the job you're being offered is a little different. You'll be with just one patient for most of the time. Will you be able to distance yourself when the time comes?'

'I'll have to,' she said simply.

'You know, then, that Sean's long-term prognosis is poor?'

'I know that; I can cope.'

'Good.' His tone altered, became less intense. 'You understand the kind of job that is being offered you? Not too much work, certainly no nightwork. Just keep an eye on Sean and make sure his grandmother doesn't worry too much. There should be plenty of time off and the house is in a very attractive part of the country.'

'It sounds ideal,' she said. 'I've fallen for the country-side already and I now realise I do need a rest.'

He pushed a piece of paper over to her. 'The conditions and rate of pay are written down here.'

She glanced at the sheet and then exclaimed, 'But I'm being paid far too much! I can't accept that.'

'The family can afford it. I'm afraid the pay's part of the package; you'll just have to accept it.' With a slightly cynical grin he said, 'Hard, isn't it?'

'Well, we'll see.'

'Is there anything else you need to know?'

Doubtfully she said, 'Well, I suppose I ought to see the grandmother first, to make sure we're going to get on. Can you tell me anything about the parents?'

He spoke harshly. 'The mother just isn't around. The father is caring—but he believes that he has to think of his work as well as his son. You'll meet him.'

52 DR RYDER AND SON

'I doubt I'll like him. If Sean was my son then I'd give up my job.'

'You can tell him. Now, is there anything else you need to know?'

She made up her mind. 'Nothing. If I can get on with the grandmother then I'll take the job.'

'The grandmother is a sweetie; I know you'll get on together.' He leaned back in his chair and said, 'I'm very pleased, Sister; you can't guess how much.' For the first time since the interview had started he smiled, and once again she marvelled at how the formidable face relaxed. This man was. . .

Then his smile slipped and he looked at her in a curiously assessing way. 'There's one thing I haven't told you. Your patient's full name is Sean Ryder. He's my son.'

CHAPTER FOUR

IT WAS a typically English view, Kate thought. A patchwork of fields stretching to low hills in the distance. There were little woods scattered haphazardly, and she could count four church steeples marking four villages. It all looked so peaceful.

She was sitting in a comfortable armchair, coffee in hand, in one of the hospital's common rooms. Her chair was pulled up to a great window and there was no one to bother her. Kate revelled in the peace, the beauty of the scene, and tried to quell her turbulent thoughts.

When Luke had spoken those terrible words there had been no possible comment. She had sat wordless, staring at his bleak face. 'Sean Ryder. He's my son.' After the silence had stretched to an almost unendurable length he had asked, 'Does this make any difference to your decision?' She had still remained speechless.

Then Marion had knocked and entered. 'If you've a minute, Luke, we could do with you on the ward.' He had stood at once and shrugged on a white coat. In a detached way Kate had registered the cartoon of Mickey Mouse embroidered on the breast pocket. He'd turned to Kate and said, 'Perhaps we could leave you in our common room for ten minutes?'

'I think that's a good idea,' she'd agreed faintly.

Four days ago her life had been simple. She'd been happy, with no problems but the day-to-day grind of work. She now realised that the shrewd Mike Hamilton had been right. She had needed a change.

But what a change! Luke Ryder had walked into her life. She had hoped, expected that he'd try to get in touch with her again. There was something between them that had to be settled. But not this way.

53

She tried to sort out the bewildering array of conflicting emotions. There was anger—she felt as if she'd been tricked, but she was still not sure how. More dominant was the bitter-sweet pleasure of seeing Luke again. Seeing his tall figure, hearing his voice so unexpectedly had been heart-shattering. But not telling her that he was Sean's father had been low! Though she could see why he'd done it—just. There was deeper anger in the fact that Luke apparently wanted her as a nurse, not a woman. But she'd taken to Sean and she'd like to see more of him.

Thoughtfully she went to the sideboard and refilled her cup. Something told her that the best thing for her now would be to leave and look for a package holiday in Spain. Something else said that there was no chance of her doing. Just for once she would act madly. She'd been the cool Sister Storm for too long.

She couldn't help looking over her shoulder when the door opened. Even though he'd said that he'd be back for her in fifteen minutes, she still felt her heartbeat accelerate. In silence she watched him pour himself coffee and then come to sit by her. For a moment he shut his eyes and she saw the fine strain lines round his mouth and at the corners of his eyes.

'A new admission,' he said flatly. 'A neonate. Mother is a drug addict with AIDS. It looks like the child is infected.'

'We've had a couple of cases like that,' she said, equally unemotionally. 'Prognosis isn't usually good.'

Neither of them said anything more. It was the kind of case you just had to cope with. There was no point in stating the emotionally obvious.

After a pause he went on, 'Then I had a quick look at Sean. I do so several times a day.'

'I'm sorry for what I said about his absent father,' she said. 'I shouldn't have judged before I knew all the facts.'

'It was a fair criticism. And I should be sorry for not

GILL SANDERSON

explaining things to you. But I wanted you to think about the job without preconceptions. I wanted *you*, both as a doctor and a father.'

Coldly she said, 'Well, thank you, Dr Ryder. I'm flattered.'

'D'you think it could be Luke again?'

She felt a fresh spurt of anger. 'I'm going to find it difficult deciding each time I speak whether you are Luke or Dr Ryder.'

'I don't think you are. You told me you could be one person on the ward and another out of it. That's what I want of you.'

Yes, she had said it. She wasn't to know how much suffering the statement would cost her.

After a pause she asked, 'One last question. You're not Sean's doctor, are you?'

'Certainly not,' he said vehemently. 'That would be foolish in the extreme. And I'm not a paediatric oncologist. I've got every faith in Marion; she's an excellent doctor. But I obviously know what's going on and she keeps me posted.' He smiled grimly. 'They say a little knowledge is a dangerous thing. A lot of knowledge can be a painful thing.'

Her heart churned with pity for him and she moved to put her hand over his. Then she decided not to. It was a gesture that might be mistaken.

He drained his coffee and swung lithely to his feet. 'If you're ready I'll take you to meet Sean's grandmother.'

'That's your mother?'

'My mother,' he agreed. 'And she really is a sweetie.' With a wink he added, 'Not like me.'

They agreed to leave her car in the hospital car park. It was now getting late and he said that whatever happened she was to stay overnight. He had to return the next day to pick up Sean. First they collected her bag and then he led her to his car—a massive Range Rover. She blinked as he opened the door and courteously helped her up.

'It's a bit big, isn't it?' she asked, thinking of her own car which was conventionally known as small.

'Winter here can be harsh. There are times when I need something like this to get through the snowdrifts.' With a muted roar they accelerated onto the main road.

The high seat enabled her to see over the tops of the roadside hedges. Sensing that she wanted to look around her, he kept quiet, and for a while she was content to enjoy the view. It was attractive countryside, cultivated but with frequent small woods. The villages they passed through were largely of mellowed red brick, with the cottages set well back from the road. She felt the peace flowing into her. Here she could unwind. But not if she was working for Luke Ryder, a voice said.

After a while he asked, 'Is there anything else you want to discuss?'

She turned to look at him. 'There's quite a lot I want to say to you. But I'd like to put it off if you don't mind.'

'That might be a good idea.'

They drove for perhaps twenty miles and dusk was drawing in as they finally reached their destination, the village of Yannthorpe. She liked it at once. A steep hill crowned by a wood stretched up behind the handful of red buildings. They turned off over a little bridge, crossing a fast-flowing stream that ran parallel to the main road. Then they pulled up outside a double-fronted building, this time of old grey stone. 'Welcome to Yann Grange,' he said.

She looked at him, puzzled. 'I thought Sean lived on a farm?'

'Originally this was Yann Grange Farm. We own all the land leading up to the top of the hill—but now it's all leased out. I didn't want to be a farmer.'

He made no move to climb out of the car, but sat as if just looking would content him for a while. She looked at his face and guessed, 'You grew up here, didn't you?'

'The first eighteen years of my life. And there have been Ryders in the house for the past two hundred years.

GILL SANDERSON

But don't start my mother on the subject unless you want to listen for hours.'

As if on cue, the front door opened and a figure appeared, bathed in the last rays of the sun. 'Luke, darling,' she called. Kate could hear an undertone of anxiety in her voice.

Luke's mother was slim, erect, her hair a mass of white curls. She was dressed in blue trousers and sweater and Kate wondered how old she was—she must be in her sixties. The thought flashed across Kate's mind that if he took after his mother Luke would grow old gracefully. Then she told herself that she wasn't really interested.

Luke had swung out of the car and was kissing his mother. Kate looked at the obvious affection between mother and son and for a moment felt desolate. She had no close family now that her father had died. It was something she missed.

'So he's still coming home tomorrow?' she heard Luke's mother ask. 'I *am* looking forward to having him back.'

'He's looking forward to coming,' Luke reassured her. 'Now I'd like you to meet Kate. She's a nurse and she'll be keeping an eye on you both. Kate, this is my mother.'

Kate stepped down from the car and took the proffered hand. In her youth Mrs Ryder must have been a beauty, and passing years had added dignity and character. Close up she was very recognisably Luke's mother. They had the same strong bone structure round the eyes, the same large, sensuous mouth.

'Kate, my dear, come inside. You must call me Lucy. Now, would you like tea straight away or would you prefer to see your room first?'

Kate was ushered through the front door.

The house was as attractive inside as it was outside. She entered a square hall, panelled in a deep red wood. Vases of flowers gave a refreshing touch of colour. She

58 DR RYDER AND SON

followed Lucy up the stairs, passing a series of water colours of country scenes.

'I've put you in here,' Lucy said, throwing open a door. 'It's at the back but that means you get the early-morning sun, and there is the view. Your bathroom's right next door.'

'This is absolutely wonderful,' Kate said sincerely. 'I love the view—and the room is so pretty.'

It was furnished with the same unerring taste that she'd seen in the hall. The furniture was old and obviously polished with love. There was the faint scent of flowers and the countryside from a bowl of pot-pourri on the dresser. A thoughtfully picked selection of books stood on a little shelf by the bed. For a moment Kate had a vision of her room at the hospital. It was clean and bright, and she'd added personal touches, but it was no more home than a hotel room would have been.

'Where will Sean sleep?' she asked briskly. It was time to remember that she was here as a professional. 'I'd like to be close to him at night.'

'I thought so. His room's right next door; come and see.'

Kate peeped in at what was definitely a young boy's room, plastered with posters and with books and games ranged on shelves. Sean was obviously interested in birds; there were numerous pictures and even a couple of models, painstakingly painted.

'I've tidied it,' Lucy confessed. 'There'll be trouble when he comes home and can't find anything. Now, do you want to freshen up and come down for a cup of tea in ten minutes?'

'I'd like that. I seem to have been travelling for a while and I'd love a shower.'

'Good. We'll be in the conservatory at the back.' Lucy turned and left.

Kate's bathroom was luxurious. The house might be old, the plumbing was certainly not. Wrapped in a large white towel, she peered round the door then scurried back to her own room. She decided not to put her trousers back on, but instead chose a pretty floral dress. For some reason she wanted to dress up, just a little. Hastily she dabbed on lipstick and went downstairs.

Lucy was alone in the conservatory at the back of the house. She smiled as Kate entered, and invited her to sit on a cushion-covered cane couch. As Lucy poured her tea Kate looked round and marvelled at the semitropical plants around her and the long vista of the garden outside. 'Who's the gardener?' she asked, though she'd already guessed the answer.

Lucy laughed. 'Well, I have a man who comes to do the heavy work. But mostly it's me. I love it.' Her face grew sad as she went on, 'Recently I've found that gardening brings me some peace. It stops me thinking about, well. . .'

'About how Sean will do?' Kate asked quietly.

'Luke is my only child and Sean is my only grandson. They both try to hide it from me, but I know they're both suffering.'

Kate knew better than to try to reassure Lucy. The cruellest treatment was to tell relations that they didn't need to worry when in fact there was every need. Instead she said, 'Try living from day to day. Don't worry about the future when you've got the present.'

'I'm sure you're right and I'll try. Luke, dear, would you like tea?'

Kate's head jerked round. She hadn't heard his approach. He too had changed his clothes. She couldn't help thinking how well he looked in whatever he dressed in—the formal consultant's suit, denim for a party, or now in dark trousers and open-necked white shirt.

'I'd love some tea,' he said, and sat beside Kate on the couch. He too had showered; she could tell by the dampness of his hair and the delicate smell of expensive soap. He sighed as he leaned back, and his bare arm grazed hers. The tiny caress made her shiver.

'Do you like the garden?' he asked, turning to her. 'My mother spends so much time in it that I tell her she should be called Eve, not Lucy.'

'It is lovely,' she said honestly. 'You know, I've never lived in a house with a garden.'

The astonishment and horror on Lucy's face was almost comic. 'Oh, dear,' she said.

'But I've always wanted one—and I do have a room full of pot plants. I was hoping you'd show me around.'

It was Luke who answered. 'There is absolutely no doubt about that. And if you show any interest—well— have you brought any gardening clothes?'

'I can improvise,' she said happily.

After a few minutes' conversation Lucy excused herself and said she'd go to see about supper. Luke remained silent by Kate's side, eyes half-closed. She was uncomfortably aware of his presence, could feel his measured breathing. She felt as if she ought to say something, but for the life of her couldn't think what.

Then he seemed to sense her mood. 'People spend too much time talking,' he said. 'Sometimes it's pleasant just to be together.' There was a pause and then he went on, in a slightly different tone. 'A lot of the time I spend with Sean he's asleep. But I like being there and I think it comforts him.'

'I'm sure it does,' she said. 'Nursing is all very well, but I think love helps an awful lot of people get better.'

'Now that is an interesting thought. D'you think we could write a joint paper on it? Love as therapy?'

She responded to his lighter tone. 'We can't write a paper yet. We haven't done enough research.'

'I'm always ready for research. Are you?' He turned to look at her, his face sardonic.

She couldn't cope with his quicksilver changes of mood, but managed to say, 'Certainly. I'm all in favour of clinical trials in hospital. Much better than in the laboratory.'

'Quite so.' He stood and walked to the window, looking out over the now shadowed garden. 'I know it's a little early to ask, but do you think you'd like to stay here with Sean and my mother?'

She replied promptly. 'Yes, if you want me and your mother will have me.' She frowned. 'But I must say this is the last thing I expected to be doing when I left Manchester this morning.'

'Do you still think you were tricked?'

'I want to stay here and nurse Sean,' she said flatly. 'But, since you ask me, yes, I do still feel I was tricked.'

There was silence for a moment. Then he said, 'I needed a nurse. When Marion mentioned your name I felt a sense of. . .rightness. I knew you were the person I wanted.'

'Just as a nurse?' she probed.

'I don't know. I——'

'Supper's ready,' said Lucy, entering the room.

She was wakened by the birds. In Manchester she slept and woke to the constant roar of traffic; here there was a chorus of wild birds from the trees at the bottom of the garden. For a while she lay there and wondered which bird sang which song. She'd ask Lucy; she would certainly know. Or she could ask Sean. Then there was a call she recognised. A cock crowed, clear as a bell.

Much to her surprise she'd slept well, better in fact than she had for weeks. More and more she was coming to agree with Mike Hamilton; she *did* need a rest. On the other hand she knew that there were questions left unanswered, problems left unsolved. They could wait; why seek out trouble? She was quite looking forward to today.

As she might have guessed, Lucy was a superb cook. Last night they'd eaten a simple meal—grilled trout and salad, followed by home-made ice cream and fresh fruit. But the polished mahogany table in the dining room had been set with silver and cut glass and illuminated by candles. She hadn't realised that elegance was so easily

DR RYDER AND SON

achieved. Luke had opened a bottle of white wine from the Loire valley and after the first mouthful she'd known that she'd never again be satisfied with bottles of plonk from the local wine store.

She'd declined coffee and come to bed early. It had been a full day. Today, she suspected, would be even more eventful.

After breakfast the three of them went to fetch Sean. Kate didn't try to help as Sean was bundled up and wheeled out to the Range Rover; she wouldn't have wanted anyone interfering in *her* ward. But she did help tuck Sean up in the back of the great car; he was now her patient.

Luke drove slowly back home and she followed easily in her little car. Once at the house Sean said that he wanted to sit for a while in the conservatory and watch the birds on the lawn. While Lucy went to fetch him some home-squeezed orange juice, Luke and Kate quietly studied the boy.

He was thin, his blue eyes looking even larger because of his hollow cheeks. To cover his baldness he wore a jaunty red football cap. She knew that his thinness was largely due to the chemotherapy he'd been undergoing—the cytotoxic drugs that attacked the body as well as the cancer.

Luke was standing just behind his son, his face impassive. She wondered exactly what he was think-ing—how he was thinking. As an oncologist he would know exactly how slim Sean's chances were. What did he feel as a father? Then he turned to her.

'It's another lovely day,' he said. 'Why don't you go for a walk through the village and up the hill? It's quite a view.'

She looked at him, confused. 'Don't you want me to help with Sean?' she asked. 'Isn't that what I'm here for?'

He smiled. 'Tomorrow I have to go back to work.

GILL SANDERSON

63

That's when you'll be really needed. I think I'll just sit here and chat with Sean for a while.'

'Are you sure there's nothing I can do?'

'Take a break while you can. I thought all nurses knew that. Ask my mother for the little book of local walks.'

Rather unwillingly she did as he said, put on a pair of boots and an anorak and borrowed a map from Lucy. Then she was striding through the village and onto the indicated path. It wound upwards through the trees—steeply. After five minutes she realised that walking through Manchester hadn't prepared her for hills like this.

Eventually, however, she reached the crest of the little hill and sat on a convenient fallen tree-trunk to get her breath back. Stretched out like a picture below her was Yannthorpe. She could easily make out the house she'd just left, with the glass conservatory behind. It gave her an odd feeling to realise that Luke and Sean were sitting in there.

It was a good time to think, so she thought. What was she going to do about Luke? It was only four days since she'd first met him, and since that time her life seemed to have been turned upside down. Mike's quiet insistence that she was exhausted, the party, knocking down Dr Norman, the trip to York and then the incredible fact that Luke wanted her as a nurse for his son. It was all too much. She needed time. However, she knew that problems shelved always grew bigger. To herself she made a promise that in exactly a week's time she'd look at the problem again—and come up with some kind of an answer. Feeling happier, she started to walk back.

The scene in the conservatory gave her an odd thrill when she walked in. Luke was sitting on the floor by Sean's chair, a pad of paper on his lap. He was trying to draw a blackbird that was perched on a bird table on the lawn outside. He wasn't doing very well.

'I think, Dad, that you've not quite got his tail feathers

right,' Sean was saying quietly. However, there was more animation in him than Kate had yet seen. Birds appeared to be the way to draw Sean out.

'Every time I think I've just about got it, he moves,' Luke said resignedly. 'Hello, Kate, did you have a nice walk?'

'I did indeed. Sean, when I was walking through the wood I saw a dark blue bird with a bright white throat. Have you any idea what it might be?'

'Blue tit,' the boy said promptly. 'He'll be looking for grubs in the tree-bark.'

She sensed rather than saw that Luke had glanced at her approvingly.

'Could I have a sheet of paper?' she asked. 'I used to like drawing at school.'

'I'm tempted to say, Take the entire pad,' Luke said grimly, 'but I'm not going to give up yet.' He tore off some sheets and handed them to her with a pencil.

For a while there was silence, broken only by the tiny hiss of pencil on paper. Sean watched carefully as the two adults concentrated on their drawing, his eyes flicking from one pad to the other. Then he spoke. 'I think Kate's is a bit better than yours, Dad.'

'What? Let's have a look.' Carefully turning his own pad face down, Luke leaned over her. She felt the warmth of his body as it touched her back, and for a moment her thoughts were miles from the bird that she was sketching. 'Kate,' he said with some surprise, 'this is really good.'

'I used to like art at school,' she said shyly. 'But, like a lot of things, I haven't had time for it recently.'

'That's a pity. Perhaps you and Sean could draw together.'

She grinned mischievously. 'That's a good idea. Now how about us looking at your drawing?'

Much to the amusement of Sean, he hastily tore off the top sheet. 'Having seen what you can do, I have no intention of exposing myself to ridicule.'

GILL SANDERSON

'I could teach you,' she teased. 'My old art teacher said anyone could learn to draw if they had patience and intelligence.'

'Patience and intelligence!'

'That's what he said. But perhaps you're too old now. Too set in your ways. I'll teach Sean instead.'

'I'll show you who's too old,' he threatened. 'I'll. . .'

Kate heard it too. The ringing of the telephone in the front hall. 'It might be one of my mother's friends,' he said.

But, of course, it wasn't. A moment later Lucy popped her head round the conservatory door. 'I'm sorry, dear,' she said, 'but it's the hospital.'

'I'll take it,' he said.

Kate had always thought that Luke's face betrayed nothing. Like so many consultants he had learned not to let his feelings show. But, when he returned, just for a moment she caught a glimpse of a maelstrom of emotions. There was anger there, and a deep sadness and pity.

'Sorry, Sean,' he said. 'I'd hoped to spend the whole day with you, but they need me back at the hospital.'

Kate winced as she saw the disappointment on Sean's thin face, but he merely said, 'All right, Dad.'

Ten minutes later Kate spoke to Luke in the hall. He was now dressed in a dark formal suit, every inch the hospital consultant.

'Perhaps I should have asked,' he said. 'You don't smoke, do you?'

She shook her head. 'Never have done, never wanted to. Why?'

'One of my patients has just been readmitted. Metastatic carcinoma of the tongue—it's spread to the lymph nodes. He's had surgery and radiotherapy but now he's bleeding again. He's been a heavy smoker all his life.'

'Can you do anything for him?' she asked, knowing the answer.

He shrugged. 'We'll try, of course. But I think I'll

DR RYDER AND SON

have to suggest to the family that he be admitted to a hospice. My SR could deal with it but I think I'd better go in.'

Kate looked at him. 'If you're treating someone,' she said, 'you feel as if in a way you're helping Sean. You don't feel so helpless all the time.'

He looked puzzled. 'Sometimes, Kate, you know what I'm thinking before I know myself. You're wonderful. Look after Sean for me.' He leaned forward, kissed her briefly on the lips then turned and slipped out of the door. Kate stood motionless, listening to the sound of the Range Rover's engine as it faded in the distance.

Kate's life fell into a routine. She prepared Sean's breakfast and helped him get up. He was too weak to move far; mostly he preferred to sit in the conservatory. They would sit and chat and she started to teach him to draw. Lucy prepared the rest of the meals and always made sure that Kate had at least one long break each day. She obviously loved Sean and wanted to do everything for him. However, she was frightened of doing something wrong and Kate could tell that she was happy that someone with medical expertise was in the house.

Every two days Kate took a blood sample and unobtrusively monitored Sean's general health. There were signs—aching legs or other pains—which were indicators of a possible relapse. Otherwise, she had little to do. She realised that she was benefiting from the easy regime just as much as Sean was.

Luke called in when he could—but it was always briefly. His face seemed to be growing thinner and she guessed that he was working far longer hours than was really healthy. Then it was Friday evening and she remembered the promise that she had made herself. After seven days—which would be on Sunday—she would sit and decide what she was going to do about her feelings for Luke. Even as she thought, the phone rang. It was Luke, for her.

'Absolutely nothing to worry about,' he said, after his usual queries about Sean, 'but Marion wants him back in hospital for thirty-six hours, for further tests. She'd like him late tomorrow evening, keep him all Sunday and discharge him Monday morning.'

'I'll get him ready,' Kate said.

'I'm desperately trying to clear my work,' he went on, 'so I shan't be home tonight. But I'll pick you both up at about seven tomorrow.'

'No problem,' she said, feeling the tiniest touch of disappointment.

'You'll have all of Sunday to yourself. Think what you'd like to do with it.'

Now she felt really disappointed.

By this time Sean was used to moving in and out of hospital, so although he'd obviously have rather stayed at home he wasn't too upset at the prospect of a short stay.

'I can practise my drawing, Kate,' was all he said.

She had him ready the following evening when Luke drew up in the Range Rover. Lucy decided not to go in this time so it was Kate who sat in the back as they journeyed back to the Wolds and Dales. She said little to Luke; he'd bought a tape of bird calls for Sean and they listened to them throughout the journey. Then Marion and the nursing team took over. Even though she'd only known him for a week it gave her an odd pang to say goodbye to Sean. She'd come to like and respect him.

It was exactly a week since she'd made this journey for the first time but it seemed like for ever. Her life in the hospital in Manchester now seemed like a distant memory. Obviously her rest-cure was working.

As he drove her back Luke said, 'I know you've had the odd couple of hours off here and there, but you've not had a day to yourself so far. What are you going to

68   DR RYDER AND SON

do tomorrow? You could visit York or Castle Howard. Or you might like to go to the coast itself.'

She muttered something about not having any firm plans yet.

After a while he went on, 'I'm going to work at home this evening and I've told the department that I'll be completely unavailable tomorrow. You might be fed up with the Ryder family by now, but if not I'd very much like it if you would spend the day with me.'

She was rather touched by the curious formality of his proposal. 'I'd be with Luke, not Dr Ryder?' she asked.

'Absolutely. And for one day we'll not mention work, cancer—not even my son, Sean. I think we both need and deserve a break.'

She knew that her cheeks were warm, and she tried to calm the feeling of excited anticipation welling within her. 'I'd like that very much—Luke,' she said. 'Where shall we go?'

He turned, and the smile that blazed on his face made her heart race. 'Leave it to me,' he said. 'I want to surprise you.'

'I love surprises,' she answered. 'At least, I think I do.'

She went to bed early that night, deciding not to look in his study and say goodnight. He'd told her that they'd make a reasonably early start. She was to wear warm, casual clothes and bring both rubber-soled shoes and walking boots.

She'd been sleeping much better since she'd got to Yannthorpe, either because of the country air or the lack of tension in her life. When someone tapped on her door next morning she was still asleep.

'Yes?' she finally called, blinking and sitting upright.

The door opened. 'Your early-morning tea, ma'am.' She blinked again. It was Luke, clad in blue trousers and a white sweater, a mug in his hand. 'I thought, since it was Sunday, you'd like to be looked after a bit,' he explained, approaching the side of her bed.

GILL SANDERSON 69

Suddenly she realised that the front of her pyjamas was open—wide open. Hastily she wriggled back under the duvet. 'You can leave it on the dresser,' her muffled voice called, 'and I'll be right down.'

'Take your time,' he said with a laugh in his voice, and she knew that her dive beneath the covers had been a little too late.

Half an hour later they were driving across the wolds, swooping up and down the bare hills, heading east. After a while, in the distance she saw the blue of the sea. They were in luck—the weather was glorious.

Finally they came to a little seaside town, its pavements thronged with holiday-makers. Kate looked at Luke curiously. This busy little town didn't seem to be the kind of place he'd want to visit.

They reached the centre of the town and turned down a ramp that led to the harbour. Then he parked inside an enclosure full of yachts on giant cradles. Here and there were men on ladders, painting their boats.

She turned to him. 'We're not going. . .?'

'Sailing? We most certainly are. Have you ever been sailing before?'

'Never.' They'd turned the corner of a giant shed and she could see the harbour ahead. The sun sparkled on the water and half a dozen white-sailed yachts were moving gently towards the harbour mouth.

'You can swim?' he asked anxiously. 'I never thought to ask.'

'I can swim,' she confirmed. 'Normally four times a week. The hospital has a pool, you know, and I do fifty lengths at a time.'

'All right, all right! Sorry I asked. I should have known better. You're just a lady superman.'

'Quite so. Is there a telephone booth handy?'

They walked down the steep slope that led to the water's edge. There was a tiny dinghy tied to an iron

70   DR RYDER AND SON

ring. He pulled at the rope, carefully handed her in then stepped in himself and started to row.

'Was it just chance there was a boat here,' she asked, 'or have you stolen it?'

He winked. 'You've found my guilty secret. I'm actually a pirate. But when I'm not pirating I phone up Hal at the marina there and ask him to get me my boat ready.'

'*Your* boat ready!'

'What use is a pirate without a boat?' In a more matter-of-fact tone he said, 'I ought to get it ready myself, I know—but time is precious.'

Just for a moment a cloud flitted over their happy mood and she remembered that this was a tiny break in the seriousness of his life. So she bounced on her seat and ripples spread from the stern of the dinghy. 'I *am* looking forward to this,' she said.

'Well, be careful or you'll have us over. And the shame of capsizing in the harbour would be too great.'

They reached a larger boat moored in the centre of the harbour, painted a dark green. Kate caught a glimpse of the name—the *Lucy R*. Luke climbed carefully aboard and then leaned over to help her. She looked around at what seemed like a chaos of ropes. 'What shall I do?' she asked doubtfully.

'For the moment, nothing. We'll get out to sea and then I'll give you a lesson.' He opened a hatch, fiddled inside and there was the burble of an engine. Leaving the dinghy tied to the moorings, the *Lucy R* motored slowly out of the harbour. There was a swell in the harbour mouth and Kate clutched the rail as the boat lifted and pounded. But soon they were well out to sea and she could feel the wind lifting her hair.

He stopped the motor and pulled at a couple of the bewildering selection of ropes. First the mainsail rose flapping in the wind, then the little jib. 'Now,' he said, 'you can feel what sailing is really like.' He tightened another rope, the sails filled with wind and the *Lucy R*.

GILL SANDERSON

leaped forward like a greyhound. Kate laughed aloud with sheer exhilaration.

Sailing was immeasurably more fun than motoring. The wind was variable; when it was stronger the boat heeled and the spray dashed backwards into her face. When the wind was light they ghosted along as if by magic.

After a while Luke got her to take the tiller and steer, and she could feel the boat responding to her hand like something alive. It was a whole new world for her and she thought that she'd like to stay out here for ever, if she could stay with Luke. They could see the town and faintly hear the noise of the funfair but she felt that they were completely alone.

They sailed for three hours. Then Luke said that they had to get back; if they missed the tide they'd have to stay out of the harbour for another twelve hours.

'I'd like that,' she said mournfully.

'There'll be another day, I promise you.'

Sadly she helped him drop the sails and they motored back into harbour.

As they walked back up the hard towards the Range Rover she saw his eyes flick towards a telephone box. She put her hand on his arm. 'I'm going to the loo,' she said. 'That'll give you five minutes to phone the hospital and ask about Sean.'

He looked at her in genuine amazement. 'How did you know I was thinking that?' he demanded.

She thought of telling him that she spent so much time thinking about him that she could guess at all of his thoughts, but decided against it. 'Woman's intuition,' she said airily. 'You've got five minutes.' She watched him set off for the kiosk.

'No problems,' he told her five minutes later as he returned. 'Marion said I should have known better than to phone.'

'We all know that doctors make lousy patients,' she said, 'but I'm glad you phoned. Now, would it be extremely impolite of me to say that the sea air has given me a vast appetite?'

'Have faith in me, woman. I've got it all arranged.'

They drove out of the now crowded town and took a narrow road that led high onto the hills. After passing through half a dozen prosperous-looking villages he pulled onto the forecourt of a pub called the Lambard Arms.

'We'll eat in the garden at the back,' he said, escorting her through a rather attractive lounge. 'You'll see why in a minute.'

She did indeed. Behind the Lambard Arms the wolds dropped steeply into the Vale of Pickering below. From the garden there was a magnificent view of the cultivated plain below and the dales in the distance.

'You don't see anything like this in London or Manchester,' he said. 'And wait till you see what we're having for lunch.'

It was in fact the simplest of meals. He ordered two ploughman's lunches. But Kate thought that she'd never tasted such a collection of breads, cheese and salad.

'It's a local secret,' Luke confided in her as she spread Stilton and apple on a crusty roll. 'None of the people here have arrived by accident. They come for George's beer and his home-baked bread.'

'I want to come again,' she gasped when she could eat no more. 'And I'll finish what I'll have to leave now.'

'You need exercise. Come on; we'll leave the car here and walk through the woods.'

He led her into a wood behind the pub and along a path that followed the crest of the wolds. They walked for perhaps half an hour and didn't meet a soul. Then he took her by the hand and turned off the path. After a few yards they broke out of the trees and were alone, high on the edge of the wolds again, with the great sweep of the valley below them.

' "What is this life if, full of care, We have no time to stand and stare?" ' he quoted. 'Would you like to rest

GILL SANDERSON 73

a while?' He sat, and she sat by his side. Neither felt any need to speak; the silence between them was companionable.

It was warm out of the shade of the trees and they were protected from any wind. After a while he pulled off his sweater and shirt and lay back on the grass, eyes closed. Covertly she admired his body, well-muscled and sinewy.

'I wish I could do that,' she said. Her wool sweater had been fine on the boat, but here it was a bit too warm.

'Why don't you?' he asked. 'There's only the two of us here; we won't be disturbed.'

'Well. . .I'd feel embarrassed.'

With a grin he said, 'I saw quite a lot of you the Wednesday before last. That blouse didn't leave much to the imagination.'

'It's different now,' she said, blushing slightly.

'Well, I'm a doctor, and, what's more, I promise not to take advantage.'

She hesitated. But the wool prickled round her neck so she crossed her arms and pulled the garment over her head. Fortunately she was wearing a sensible bra—one she wore on the ward.

The sun and the slightest of breezes on her skin were like champagne. For a while she remained sitting, her arms crossed semi-defensively in front of her, but Luke didn't even open his eyes.

She felt sleepy. The early start, the sea air and the meal were taking their toll. Luke was already half-asleep; she could hear his breathing and see the movement of his chest. Gently she lay down by his side, not touching, and closed her own eyes. She too drifted off into a half-sleep.

She could tell when he woke. He didn't move, but his breathing changed and she felt his relaxed muscles tense a little. 'Do we have to go?' she asked, without opening her eyes.

'Soon, I think. This spot will be in shadow soon.'

74   DR RYDER AND SON

'Pity. I like it here.' After a while she went on, 'Are you happy?'

'Yes. It's been a good day.'

'You can only be happy one day at a time,' she said, 'so make the most of it.'

'I will.' She guessed that in spite of his promise he was thinking about Sean, and a great wave of sympathy washed over her. On impulse she leaned over and kissed him, on the lips, but quickly.

His eyes flashed open. 'That was very nice,' he said, 'but what about taking advantage?'

'I'm entitled to, you're not.'

'So I can't kiss you back?'

'Certainly not,' she said primly. 'You gave your word—as a doctor.'

'That's not fair!' he growled.

'It's an unfair world. Come on; we should be getting back.' She rolled to her feet and extended a hand to pull him up.

She'd forgotten her half-naked top, and only when his eyes burned across her did she remember and blush. 'Here,' he said, and offered her her sweater.

They walked back through the woods hand in hand. 'Thank you for a lovely day,' she said as they neared the car.

'One day at a time,' he said. 'And I shall remember this one.'

CHAPTER FIVE

SOMETHING happened as they drove back home.

At first Kate was perfectly content, watching the sun-dappled landscape fly past, listening to the tape of Lena Horne on the car stereo. She'd found that she could spend long periods of time with Luke without saying anything. They didn't need to speak to enjoy each other's company.

But then the atmosphere changed. It might have been the set of his body, the way he was frowning or the angry way he changed the tape. Whatever it was, she felt the peace and happiness of the past few hours slipping away.

She remembered that a week ago she'd promised herself that today she'd think about her situation, try to take control of it. Because Luke had taken her out for the day she'd postponed any decision-taking; perhaps she should start now.

Leaning forward, she switched off the stereo. He glanced at her, surprised, but said nothing. Carefully she tried to marshal her thoughts.

'There's something that's worrying you,' she said. 'I think it's something to do with me. Will you tell me what it is?'

'How d'you know something's worrying me?'

She sighed. 'Luke, I deserve better than this. For some reason what's been a wonderful day has changed. Now, tell me if there's anything wrong and we can talk about it.'

They were driving along the ridge of a hill just before dropping into the vale below. Woods lined the road. He slowed and turned onto a forest track. After a few yards they came to a bench with a view across the vale. He

76 DR RYDER AND SON

stopped the car and got out. 'I don't think we ought to talk about this in the car,' he said grimly.

She climbed out, fearing what he was going to say.

He didn't take her arm to walk her to the bench, and when he sat down he took his place as far from her as he could. She thought of moving towards him, then decided not to. Let him make the first move.

When he started talking he didn't look at her, but stared fixedly across the vale, as if there were consolation in the distance.

'This is difficult,' he said jerkily, 'and if I offend you it's the last thing I want to do. But I've been thinking a lot about you. It seems that I've known you for ever—you've fitted into my life with Sean and Lucy and it's only been twelve days.'

'You found me on the ward,' she said.

'Fighting like a lion. I was impressed. The contrast between that sweet face and the absolute determination to do what you thought was right.'

'Then there was the party,' she went on bitterly. 'I felt jealous when a woman phoned you and you left at once.'

'That was Marion. She phoned to say some test results on Sean had just come in; they were satisfactory. I've asked her to let me know the minute she learns anything, good or bad.'

'Good news! Why didn't you come back to celebrate?' She was angry now.

'The phone call reminded me I had responsibilities. I very much wanted to spend more time with you, but I didn't know where it would lead.'

Kate wanted to say that she felt that she ought to have been consulted before he'd made any decisions. But wisely she said nothing.

'I was—I am very attracted to you. Physically I think you're wonderful, but I suppose I've known physically attractive women before. It's what's underneath that counts. It's the real you that I. . .that fascinates me.'

GILL SANDERSON

After a pause he said, 'And I think you feel something like that about me.'

'It's possible,' she lied through dry lips.

He reached over and briefly clasped her hand. When she tried to clutch his in return he pulled away.

'I've got a son who has cancer. We both know what his chances of survival are—who better? Every day of remission is just to be enjoyed, but at the same time it makes the fear of his slipping into relapse even greater. With me comes Sean. If you feel for me you will feel for him. And I will not subject another person to what I feel.'

'But I feel for Sean already,' she cried. 'Surely you can see that?'

'I know you do but you're his nurse. And I've never met one as competent and as caring as you. But I believed you when you said a good nurse has to be able to switch off when she leaves the ward. That's what you'll have to do with Sean.'

'What are you really saying?' she asked dully. 'You're not really talking about Sean.'

'No, I'm talking about us. I can't, I won't offer you any commitment. I dearly hope we can be friends. But we'll never be lovers.'

The cold words hung between then with a deadening finality.

'Don't I get a chance of saying anything?' She could tell by his adamant tone what the answer would be, but she had to ask.

'No. It's a decision only I can make and I've made it. And it hurts, Kate, so please don't make it any worse by arguing.'

A thousand arguments and pleas flooded through her mind but, looking at his stone-hard face, she knew that they'd all be useless. She reached over to him, hugged him briefly and said, 'Let's go back.'

They were only ten minutes' drive from home. As they neared Yannthorpe she asked, 'What are you going to do tonight?'

78 DR RYDER AND SON

He turned and smiled at her, and her heart nearly burst when she saw the pain in it. 'Well, I was going to have a civilised, idle evening with you,' he said. 'A bottle of wine and a relaxed chat. But as it is I guess I'll go to my study and work.'

'It might be a good idea,' she agreed. She knew how she would feel.

That night she went to bed early, but she couldn't sleep. Her body was satisfactorily tired but her mind was in tumult. First she tried to read, then she switched off the bedside light and lay staring at the stars framed by her half-open bedroom curtains.

She thought about what Luke had said. She could respect his feelings—even sympathise with them. But what about *her* feelings?

She'd been in Yannthorpe only a week or so, and had come to love it. She'd have liked to stay here for ever. The feelings of stress she'd had when she'd left Manchester were slipping away. Mike had been right: she was near to exhaustion.

Should she leave Manchester? She now realised that it had been a depressing place for her; the memories of her father's death were too intimately wrapped together with her work.

It was no good; she couldn't sleep. Then below she heard the stealthy sound of someone opening the conservatory door. Swinging her legs out of bed, she hurried to peer through the gap in the curtains.

It was Luke. Wineglass in hand, he wandered across the grass and sat in a rustic chair to stare at the sky.

He too couldn't sleep; she knew exactly what he was feeling. She was feeling it herself. For a mad moment she considered hurrying downstairs and throwing herself into his arms.

She would do it! She reached for her dressing gown. And at that moment the conservatory door opened again. 'Luke? Are you all right?' Another figure walked onto the lawn; it was Lucy. Kate stood numbly a moment. Then she went back to bed and pulled the pillow over her ears.

Next morning they went early to pick up Sean. Since Kate was going to bring Sean back in her car she and Luke didn't travel together and she decided that she was thankful for this. A journey in near-silence or one filled with meaningless chatter would have been unendurable. So she drove behind the Range Rover and noticed that he held back his normal speed so that she could keep up. For some reason this consideration irritated her.

Sean was ready to come home. The effects of the chemotherapy were slowly wearing off, and he was gaining weight and strength. He took more interest in the world around him.

Luke and Kate watched as he was eased, like a big cocoon, into the back of her car. She found that she could speak to Luke quite easily if the subject was patient care—neutral ground as it were.

'He's going to get bored if we're not careful,' she said. 'I think I'd better start him on some lessons.'

Luke turned his eyes from his son. 'Could you do that?'

'Quite easily. I've done it before. If necessary I'll pop into the village school and ask to borrow a couple of books; I'm sure they wouldn't mind.'

'It's very good of you, Kate. You're supposed to be his nurse, not his tutor.'

'I'll enjoy it,' she said thinly. 'Just call it part of the overall patient care.'

He said nothing but watched as the two hospital nurses pulled the seat belt round Sean's blanket-clad form and carefully clipped him in. 'All yours now,' one said brightly. 'Keep smiling, Sean; we'll miss you.' Then they hurried back to the ward.

80   DR RYDER AND SON

'I'll phone every day, of course,' Luke said abruptly, 'but I've got work to do here.'

'I'm sure we'll manage.' The distance was between them again; the intimacy and pleasure they'd taken in each other's company yesterday seemed a thousand years away. She waited until he'd had one last word with his son. Then she climbed into the driver's seat with a brief meaningless smile. 'Goodbye, Luke.'

She drove slowly down the hospital drive, her eyes turning constantly to her mirror. He didn't move. Her last view was of his tall, dark-suited figure standing like a great god outlined against the line of the hills. She blinked, telling herself that the tears came from the wind.

All that day and the next a blustering wind blew down from the hills and Kate decided that it was too cold to take Sean for the short walks that she had planned. Instead she took down a few books and tried to find out exactly what he knew.

Most large hospitals had an education section, with teachers for children who needed long-term treatment. Too often, however, children in cancer wards were far too ill to benefit from what was available

To her surprise she found that Sean wasn't too far behind. He would much rather read than watch television. He told her that his father had spent many hours after his first spell in hospital teaching him maths and English. When she heard this she felt a pang of sympathy.

Luke rang to talk to Sean each night. When the time approached for his call, Kate was happy to see Sean getting more and more excited. There was another, less agreeable feeling that she couldn't at first put a name to. To her horror she realised that it was jealousy, and promptly felt ashamed of herself.

Sean was fascinated by birds, and she decided that this would be a useful way of improving his English. They started to keep a bird diary, with observations and

GILL SANDERSON 81

drawings. Then Wednesday dawned a beautiful, bright day and Lucy came in from the village with some news.

'Mr Harris says there's an owl in the long barn behind the bakery. He saw it when he was parking his car last night.'

That did it. First they had to look at the bird book to decide what kind of bird it might be. Then they had to go to the long barn.

It was the first time for quite a while that Sean had been able to walk outside. Their progress was slow, but he obviously enjoyed the unaccustomed exercise. She decided that they'd have to come out more often.

He was still very susceptible to infection and was not to meet too many people. When they got to the baker's she told him to wait outside on a bench while she went in to ask if they could look in the barn.

Permission was readily granted. Then when she came out she saw a car drawn up on the opposite side of the road from Sean, a battered old Land Rover. The driver, a man aged about sixty, was staring across at Sean with what she thought was a wistful expression. Kate just had time to register bright blue eyes and a white beard. Then the man saw her coming and slowly drove away.

'Who was that in the car, Sean?' she asked cautiously.

'I didn't see anybody. Look, there's starlings in the trees over there. We'll have to put them in the book. Can we go in the barn now?'

'Mr Harris says we can look as often as we want. Come on.'

There were plenty of places where the owl could be nesting, but all were inaccessible. Sean looked around excitedly. 'Could we come and stay up all night, Kate? With sandwiches and things? We'd be sure to see him then!'

'Perhaps your dad will bring you in a month or two. For the moment you need to be in bed at night.'

'I'd love to have an owl in my bird book. Can we draw one?'

82   DR RYDER AND SON

'We can certainly do that.' As it was his first trip out, she decided that they'd better go straight back.

After a light lunch Sean usually had a sleep. Kate was chatting to Lucy in the kitchen when she remembered what had happened outside the baker's. 'Lucy,' she said, 'do you know a man of about sixty—got a white beard and very blue eyes? I saw him looking at Sean. He looked rather sad.'

For a moment Lucy stopped drying the dish in her hands. Then she said, 'That would be Harry Wentworth. He's Luke's divorced wife's father.'

'Sean's grandfather?' Kate probed delicately.

'I suppose so. Well, in fact I know so. Look, Kate, I think this is Luke's story to tell. He's coming tonight so you can ask him about it.'

Kate frowned. 'Would it be better if I didn't mention it? I don't want to pry, you know.'

Lucy rubbed furiously at the dish. 'No,' she said. 'I think you should tell him. He's my son and I love him, but he can be a stubborn so-and-so at times.' She placed the super-dried dish in the cupboard and then went on, 'But he can be very kind as well.'

Kate didn't know what to make of this. She thought of his mother's comments on Luke—stubborn but can be very kind. Well, yes, she thought. That's about right. And dangerously easy to love.

Luke hadn't been home for two days; the work at hospital had been mounting up. When he came that evening she tried to stay in the background, but he came to find her anyway. She thought that his face was thinner, and wondered if she was the cause; perhaps he was feeling the same pain as she was. But then she remembered his son and felt guilty again.

'I thought I'd leave you to have dinner with your son and mother,' she said. 'You must have things to talk about.'

GILL SANDERSON

'You're one of the family; you must join us. Besides, Sean would miss you.'

It's not Sean I want to miss me, she thought, but came to the dinner table, knowing that it would be a bitter-sweet pleasure. But it wasn't too bad, and after a while she managed to persuade herself that perhaps indeed she was one of the family.

After the meal Sean had to get his bird book out and show his father what he had done over the past three days.

'This is very good indeed, Sean,' Luke said, examining the drawing of an owl and reading how Sean hoped in time to be able to see it.

'I did it all myself,' Sean said importantly. Then, with the honesty that Kate had come to love in him, he said, 'But perhaps Kate helped me quite a lot.'

Luke's eyes flicked up to see her eyes fastened on him. For a moment they gazed at each other and it seemed as if there was a communion there that went beyond words. Then he said, 'A teacher as well as a nurse, Kate? What else can you do?'

'You'll never know,' she said flippantly.

'I suppose not.' Her heart wrenched at his quiet words.

Later that night she and Luke put Sean to bed and then Lucy excused herself, saying that she felt tired. Kate was torn two ways. She wanted to avoid the pain of being with Luke—but wanted the pleasure of being with him too. That is just ridiculous, she thought wryly. In the end he said that he was going to have a whisky and would she join him. 'Just a small one,' she said.

They sat, as ever, in the conservatory. Before the silence could get too long and oppressive she thought of the morning's events. 'Luke,' she said, 'this morning in the village I saw a man staring at Sean. Lucy said he might be Sean's grandfather.'

She waited anxiously for Luke's reply, hoping that she hadn't upset him.

'Harry Wentworth, my ex-father-in-law,' he said after

84 DR RYDER AND SON

a while. 'He's quite a nice chap. Technically, Sean's grandfather.'

'Technically? I only saw him for a minute but he was looking rather sad. I know it's no business of mine but perhaps you ought to tell me a little. I mean, just in case Sean ever asks.'

At first she thought that he wasn't going to reply. He added more whisky to his glass, asking her by a quirk of his eyebrows if she too wanted a refill. She shook her head.

Then he said flatly, 'Sean's mother, my ex-wife, is Maria Wentworth.'

Kate blinked. 'The Maria Wentworth! The show-jumper?'

'The very same.'

Kate's brain was a whirl. She didn't often read women's glossy magazines, but even she knew who Maria Wentworth was. There was no end of pictures of her hard beauty, usually taken while she was still on her horse. She was not just a fashion-plate, though. It was thought that she would represent Great Britain in the next Olympics.

'The family stud is about fifteen miles away,' Luke went on dispassionately. 'I've known Maria since she was a little girl. Anyway, we got married. We were both far too young and it was entirely my fault. I should have known better. Maria just wasn't suited to be the wife of a doctor in London, and she spent an awful lot of time up here.'

'You don't have to tell me if you don't want to,' Kate said, though she was both horrified and fascinated.

'I want to. We then had Sean——largely, I suspect, because she was bored. She doted on him at first, but when he was demanding she just couldn't cope. Said she was a horsewoman, not an unpaid skivvy. Two years ago Sean was diagnosed as having acute lymphoblastic leukaemia and she went completely to pieces. We had a series of screaming rows when she accused me of bringing home the infection from work. And nothing could change her mind.'

He sipped more whisky and she could tell that, although his voice was as controlled as ever, there was a deep thread of anger underneath.

'I suppose I should be able to understand; after all, it's something I've come across before. Eventually she rejected me and Sean completely. She just couldn't cope with the idea of his illness. She never wanted to see him or me again. Well, I arranged counselling sessions for her but they did no good. So we got divorced. And I said it had to be a complete clean break. I hired the best lawyers to ensure she never had any claim on Sean or me. We haven't spoken in over a year. I understand she's married another doctor—this time a plastic surgeon with a very lucrative practice in Harley Street.'

'And you divorced her family along with your wife?'

'Apparently. It seemed a good idea at the time. Maria's mother, Molly, was just an older version of Maria. She died in a car crash about a year ago. She never wanted us to get married. But Harry's quite a pleasant chap; I liked him.'

Kate sipped at her glass and discovered that it was empty. 'Do you think I could have another very small drink?' she asked. 'You've given me quite a lot to think about.'

He poured her the requested small drink, and she was pleased that he didn't try to force her to have more than she wished.

It was a while before she could formulate her next question, but eventually she tentatively asked, 'Do you think your—experiences with Maria have affected your view of all women?'

'D'you mean my view of you?' he asked directly, and she could only nod.

'Kate, you're a creature from a different world from Maria. But I suppose you're right. I just don't trust any woman now.'

DR RYDER AND SON

Desperately she wanted to tell him that he was wrong to judge all women by just one, but she didn't know how.

He went on, 'You've met parents whose children have cancer. It's terrifying for them. The interesting thing is that often the toughest break under the strain. And the most unlikely manage to cope.'

She had to agree. The complete rejection of a child with cancer was not entirely unknown. But still. . .'I don't think many of us are asked to take more than we can bear,' she said.

'Perhaps not. You know, Kate, if you weren't a magnificent nurse you could be a counsellor. I've said things to you I've admitted to nobody else.'

'Well, thank you,' she said. And once again, if only for a while, there was that sense of unspoken warmth between them, silent but deeply felt.

'What about Sean's grandfather?' she asked eventually. 'Do you think he'd like to meet his grandson?'

'I'm sure he would. He doted on Sean as a baby, but when it came to trouble I suppose he thought he had to support his wife and daughter. I don't suppose I made it easy for him either.'

'Could I phone him and ask if we could call round?'

He didn't answer and the silence between them lengthened. She determined not to speak first. Then he said, 'You're Sean's nurse. If you think it would be of benefit to him, then certainly you can phone Harry.'

'You'd give me that responsibility? You want me to decide?'

'I do. I believe in giving as much responsibility as possible. The decision is now yours to make; you must live with the consequences.'

He stood, placed his glass on a table and walked to her chair. She stared as if hypnotised as he bent over her. He touched his lips to her forehead and the tiny caress burned like fire. 'Goodnight, dear Kate,' he said.

When he'd left the room she still sat there, waiting for the storm of emotions to subside. Didn't he know

GILL SANDERSON 87

what he was doing to her, what her feelings were? Perhaps he did. And she suspected that he felt the same way.

Luke left very early the next morning, before she was out of bed. She resolved to think of other things, and consulted Lucy. Lucy very much approved, so with some trepidation Kate phoned the Wentworth Stud. Harry Wentworth was available.

'I'm the nurse in charge of Sean Ryder,' Kate said. 'I saw you looking at him yesterday. Would you like to come round and see him?'

The voice on the other end of the line was full of feeling. 'I would indeed,' Harry Wentworth said. 'But first—does Luke know you're asking me?'

'He knows,' Kate said, 'and he's very happy about it.'

'When can I come?'

Harry's visit was a great success. He brought pictures of the horses he had trained and promised that when Sean was stronger he could come to the stud for a ride. Very wisely, he realised that Sean was still not very strong and so he didn't stay too long. Kate thought that he was a charming man and wondered if his daughter was like him. Then she told herself that it was none of her business.

Before he left he had a moment alone with her. 'You know about Luke and my daughter, then?' he asked.

'Luke did explain a bit of the situation,' she said tactfully. 'I needed to know because of Sean.'

'That's fair enough. I always liked Luke—will you thank him for this chance? And thank you too.'

'We'll see you again soon,' she promised.

That evening she sat musing in the garden. Sean was already in bed; she always took care to make sure that he didn't get overtired. She was pleased that she'd invited Harry; she thought that both he and Sean would benefit from seeing each other. I can help other people with

88 DR RYDER AND SON

their lives, she thought. Why can't I do something about my own?

It would soon be the end of her second week here. A week after that and she'd be back at work. She felt better for the rest, for the comparatively light workload. With every day the realisation came clearer—she had been exhausted. It was a danger that she'd look out for and avoid in the future.

What future? Luke had made it abundantly clear that there was no future with him. Yet a future without him seemed bleak in the extreme. She thought that Maria Wentworth must have been incredibly stupid to give up someone like Luke. And she thought that he was wrong when he refused to share his life with anyone else because of Sean. But she knew that once Luke made up his mind nothing could change it. It was one of the things she loved—and hated—about him.

Gloomily she decided that she'd go back to Manchester but then make a break. She'd find another job, perhaps abroad. She'd start her life afresh. Her mind was made up—but she didn't feel much better for it.

Dusk was falling as she went back into the house to the kitchen for a drink. Lucy was sitting in the armchair in the corner of the kitchen, clutching her left shoulder with her right hand. Something about the way her body was slumped alerted Kate at once.

'Are you all right, Lucy?'

When Lucy managed to speak her voice was weak, and as Kate got nearer she could hear the sound of rasping breath.

'I thought it was indigestion at first, dear,' Lucy managed to gasp, 'though I don't normally suffer from it. First there was a pain over my heart but now it seems to have moved to my shoulder here.'

Swiftly Kate snapped on the light. Lucy was obviously in pain and Kate could see her chest rising and falling at what seemed to be a tremendous rate.

Tears trickled down Lucy's face. 'I was thinking of

Sean and Luke,' she mumbled. 'There seems no end to it. I love them. . .'

'Don't talk, Lucy,' Kate said reassuringly. 'You're going to be all right. Just let me take your pulse.'

The moment she felt Lucy's pulse Kate knew that she was in trouble. It was fast—incredibly fast. She looked at her watch and counted the heartbeats over fifteen seconds. Twenty-nine! That was a pulse rate of over a hundred and sixteen. At Lucy's age her heart couldn't stand that for long.

Hastily Kate eased Lucy into a semi-recumbent position. 'You'll feel better like that,' she said. Then she snatched the telephone from the wall and dialled 999.

'Heart attack,' she told the controller after giving the address. 'We must have an ambulance with paramedics.' Then she rushed and opened the front door.

As she came back to Lucy what she feared happened. There was a last rasping breath and then nothing further. Lucy's overworked heart had stopped.

Oxygen to the brain, Kate thought. She knew her chances of restarting Lucy's heart were slim, but if she could keep oxygenated blood circulating then Lucy's brain might not be damaged. First, she eased the old lady onto the kitchen floor. She knelt by Lucy's head and opened her mouth to check for dentures and to make sure that she hadn't swallowed her tongue. Then she squeezed the nose and bent the head back so that the air would have a clear passage. The drill was simple. Mouth-to-mouth resuscitation: four breaths of air and then the weight of the body, stiff-armed, onto the heart, to make it pump.

Kate blew—one. . .two. . .three. . .four—then moved and pushed at Lucy's heart. She'd practised this on a life-sized doll in the hospital.

There was no sign of Lucy's heart starting to beat. All the work was done by Kate. After five minutes her arms were weary and she felt dizzy. Her cramped position was not a good one for working in. She blew again—one...two...three...four—wondering how long the ambulance would be. If there was someone else here they could take over. For a moment she considered leaving Lucy and going for help from a neighbour. But Lucy couldn't be left. Thank goodness Sean was asleep.

Time passed. It seemed such a simple movement, so easy to do. Her arms now felt as if they had hot wires threaded through them and she felt nearer to collapse than she did after a hard game of squash. For a moment of panic she wondered if she'd be able to keep this up. She'd have to! Lucy remained motionless.

All her consciousness was focused on her work. It came almost as a shock when the front doorbell rang and someone shouted hello from the hall. 'Down here,' she managed to call. Then two green-suited paramedics, one man, one woman, were in the kitchen with her and she knew in a moment that she'd be able to relax.

'Heart attack,' she gasped. 'About fifteen minutes ago. I've kept this up since then. I'm a nurse.'

'Keep going just for a minute, love,' the man said, and bent down to check the carotid artery in Lucy's neck. Meanwhile his companion carefully eased up Lucy's sweater to fix on the three leads from her monitor.

'Ventricular fibrillation,' she reported after scanning the screen. She ran back to the ambulance to return a moment later with the defibrillator. 'We'll have to shock her,' she said. 'Could you stand back, miss, please?'

Kate knew that these people were well trained; the best thing to do was let them work as a team. She went to the far side of the kitchen to be out of the way, her agonised muscles thankful for the respite.

'You've done a good job,' the man said. 'I don't think I could keep that up for fifteen minutes.'

As he spoke he was helping his partner. The two gel pads of the defibrillator were held against Lucy's naked chest.

Lucy's body convulsed as the charge contracted her muscles. The man put his hand to the side of her neck, feeling again for the carotid artery. 'I think we've got an output,' he said, with guarded optimism.

For perhaps a minute they waited, motionless. Kate could see colour returning to Lucy's cheeks, the gentle rise and fall of her chest. She was breathing again. Perhaps all could be well.

When they thought it safe to do so the two paramedics went to fetch their trolley. Once in the ambulance Lucy was fitted with an endotracheal tube to maintain her airway and given an oxygen mask. She was efficiently cannulated for IV access. Adrenalin was quickly administered. Lucy was now half-awake so she was given soluble aspirin.

Kate had seen and done all this before, but only in a hospital ward where everything was to hand. She marvelled at the efficiency of this pair.

Eventually they were ready. They asked Kate if she wanted to ride to the hospital with them.

She shook her head. 'I'd like to——but I have a patient upstairs. Are you going to casualty in the Wolds and Dales?'

'That's our hospital. We'll be there in half an hour.'

'This lady's son works there. I'll phone him and I'm sure he'll meet you.' She gave a few more details and then watched as Lucy was lifted into the ambulance.

Kate watched the ambulance drive expertly out of the village and then walked back into the house. It had been an exciting half-hour. She knew that Lucy was in good hands; with any luck she should now be out of danger.

Kate slipped upstairs and peered in at Sean. He was sleeping peacefully. For some reason it gave her a feeling of relief.

Luke had given Kate a phone number for emergencies and told her that he could be contacted on it at any time, day or night. She guessed what effect the call would have on him but there was nothing she could do. 'Could you ask Dr Ryder to ring home immediately, please?'

She sat by the phone. She felt chilled, and was aware

DR RYDER AND SON

that her blouse was sticking to her after her exertions. The phone rang. 'Kate?' His voice was calm but even in the one word she could sense the fear underneath.

'Luke, it's not Sean; he's fine. But it is bad news. Your mother had a heart attack. It was serious but she seems to be a bit better now and she's on her way to your casualty department by ambulance.'

There was still that iron self-control. 'How serious was it, Kate?'

'Well, I had to give her heart massage and keep her breathing going till the paramedics arrived.'

'I see. She was lucky you were there. My son and now my mother. We do seem to be keeping the doctors busy.' It was a slight, throw-away remark. But just for once Kate could tell the anguish that he was going through.

'Luke, I'm so sorry,' she said, feeling that there was nothing adequate that she could say.

'I know, Kate.' He paused a moment and then said, 'Kate, first of all, thanks. I'll go down to Casualty now and wait for her. Are you all right for the evening with Sean?'

'No problem at all. You will phone and tell me how Lucy is?'

'Of course. Thanks again, Kate.' He rang off.

For a moment she didn't have the strength to move. She sat there in the hall, thinking about the brief conversation with Luke. It had been short, efficient, and could have taken place between two complete strangers. She wondered what could pierce that steel wall that Luke had erected round his emotions. It didn't seem to be her. She struggled to her feet and went upstairs to have a shower.

Sean took the news that his grandmother had gone to hospital well. He had travelled so much to and from hospital himself that he didn't think it too strange that she should have done the same. He accepted Kate's reassurance that it was nothing much, that she'd gone for a check-up, quite happily. She, however, was waiting for the next telephone call.

It came after an hour and it wasn't from Luke. He'd asked one of the junior doctors to phone Kate. Perhaps it was the sensible thing to do, but she would have liked a personal call.

'Dr Ryder asked me to say that his mother is definitely out of danger and it doesn't look like there'll be any serious long-term effects. He's sitting with her now, or he would have phoned himself. He's going to come home this evening——but he says it might be very late, so you're to go to bed.'

'I'll do that,' Kate said, knowing that there was no chance of it. 'Tell him that Sean and I are quite all right.'

It was well past midnight when she finally heard the front door open. She was sitting in the kitchen, and walked into the hall to meet him.

His face looked even thinner, the cheekbones showing high over the slightly unshaven jaws. There were black smudges under his eyes. Through sheer compassion at his weariness she put her arms round him and hugged him. 'I'm glad you're here,' she said simply. 'Come into the kitchen and tell me how Lucy is.'

He smiled, and she wondered if he knew what effect that had on her. 'Basically, Lucy is all right,' he said.

Guessing that he'd hurry home without eating, she'd made him a salad. Three of Mr Harris the baker's excellent rolls were warming gently in the oven. 'What would you like to drink?' she asked. 'Tea, coffee or. . .?'

'I think ''or'',' he said. 'I'll open a bottle of burgundy if you'll join me in a drink. Kate, you shouldn't have gone to all this trouble.'

'You haven't eaten, have you?' she asked, pulling the rolls out of the oven. 'So sit down.'

First, however, as she might have guessed, he ran upstairs to look at the sleeping Sean. Then he came back to the kitchen, carrying a bottle.

94 DR RYDER AND SON

'We should wait for it to breathe,' he said. 'But tonight we won't.'

She told him to have his meal before talking, and by the delight he took in her simple salad it was obvious that he hadn't eaten for quite a while. Then finally he chose an apple and carved himself a chunk of Brie. 'Let's go into the conservatory,' he said. 'And we can relax.'

They walked through and, wineglass in hand, she sat to listen to him. 'First of all,' he started, 'Lucy is fine. As you thought, she had a heart attack, probably brought on by strain and worry.' A frown clouded his tired face. 'I should have been on the lookout for that,' he said. 'I tend to forget that not all people are as tough as me.'

Some people *are* as tough as you, she wanted to say, but managed to keep quiet.

'The cardiologist is a good pal of mine and he says there's no great reason to worry—now. A week or so's bedrest and then convalescence for a month or so. She's got a younger sister in Llandudno who'll be only too pleased to fuss over her. And afterwards she'll have to take beta blockers to keep her pulse down.'

'That still leaves us with a lot of problems,' Kate said.

'It does indeed.' He looked at her levelly, keeping his glass touching his lip, so half his face was hidden and she was unable to decide what he was thinking. 'You know that the paramedics report to the Casualty doctor as a matter of course. It turns out that you saved Lucy's life.'

'I'm a nurse,' she mumbled. 'That's what we do.'

'Not all nurses could do what you did, Kate. I just want you to know how grateful I am.'

She could think of nothing to say. It wasn't his gratitude she wanted.

'We contracted for you to look after Sean for three weeks,' he went on, 'and you're expected back at Manchester a week on Monday.'

She nodded. 'I needed a rest. And, don't laugh, but I think I've had one.'

GILL SANDERSON

He winced. 'If this is a rest then your work must be quite something.'

'I enjoy my work. But I was just thinking that I'd got a bit stale. When I get back to Manchester I'll probably look round for a new job.'

'You mean that?'

'Well, yes,' she said defensively, hoping that he wouldn't question her too closely as to why she wanted to move on.

'That makes this easier for me. Kate, to start with you should know that I'm a bit like your pal Mike Hamilton. I've got the reputation of being manipulative, unscrupulous and doing anything to get my own way.'

'Surprise me,' she muttered.

'So I'm now going to try to manipulate you. In a fortnight I'm going to San Francisco for an oncological conference lasting a fortnight. I just can't miss it; I'm giving one of the lead papers and there are people there I have to talk to. I had hoped Sean would be well enough to stay with Lucy. Now Lucy won't be well enough to stay with Sean. I've no right to ask this, but if I can square it with your hospital, will you look after Sean for another month?'

She gazed at him, mouth open. Nothing had prepared her for this. In the back of her mind she had known that something would have to be done about Sean. But for the moment she had worried solely about Lucy. 'Could——could you arrange it with the hospital?' she asked.

'I suspect that would be the least of our problems. Look, Kate, it's late at night and I've sprung this on you. Think about it for a day or so. I don't want you saying yes to something you'll regret.'

'All right, I'll think about it overnight.' But even as she spoke she knew that there was no need. Sean was now far more than her patient. She loved the time she spent with him. And she knew that she was the best person for this job; she was helping him in his recovery. She wanted to stay with him.

There was another reason. If there was the prospect of staying near Luke she'd take it. She also guessed that it would be something she'd regret.

CHAPTER SIX

LUKE rose early the next morning but she was up before him. She knew that he wouldn't want a large breakfast so she made him coffee and toast. Once again they sat at the kitchen table. 'I keep on saying this, Kate,' he said, 'but you shouldn't have bothered.'

'I'm happy to. Besides, I needed to talk to you. I've made my decision; I'd like to stay and look after Sean. I've got very attached to him and I think my staying would be the best thing in the circumstances.'

'You've decided so quickly? Are you sure you've had enough time to think?'

'I've had enough time. In fact I've been awake most of the night.'

He looked uncomfortable. 'Kate, that was the last thing I wanted.'

'I know that. Now, there's one condition. I'm a nurse, and I like to think I've got a reputation for professionalism. I want to hang onto that reputation. I don't want to leave my ward inadequately staffed and I don't want anyone in my old hospital thinking that I've left because I'm. . .because I'm. . .' She floundered, not quite knowing how to phrase what she was thinking.

'You've left because you're chasing a handsome young doctor?' he supplied sardonically. 'Kate, you flatter me.'

'Well, something like that,' she muttered. 'And I'm not flattering you. But you know what hospital gossip is like.'

'I do indeed, Kate, but I don't think you need worry. I'll phone Mike Hamilton and get him to have a word with the hospital manager. If there's goodwill all round it's usually possible to arrange these things.'

98   DR RYDER AND SON

'That's settled, then,' she said flatly.

'Don't you want to talk about conditions...pay... anything like that?'

'I'm not all that bothered. You may have your faults but you've always been more than generous with me.'

'A compliment,' he muttered, 'even if a grudging one.' He looked at her silent figure a moment and then said, 'There's something else you want to say, isn't there, Kate?'

'Yes. I am very fond of Sean and I'm looking forward to seeing more of him. But you know, don't you, that that's only half the reason I'm taking this job?'

There was silence. Then he said slowly, 'Yes, I know. You're taking this job partly so you can be near me. And I've an awful suspicion that I offered it to you partly so I could be near you. But it just won't do. I won't— I can't—I daren't start another relationship.'

She stared at him without speaking.

He went on, 'I do feel bad about the way I'm treating you. But I'm basically selfish—if not for myself, then for my patients and my son. And for them I'm willing to take advantage of you.'

He stood and grabbed his briefcase. 'You can still change your mind, you know. I'll see you tonight.'

'I've already given you my decision. It stands.' She watched him walk out of the door.

Kate had lived in town all her life; she was still getting used to the uncanny way that news travelled through the countryside. Lucy had been taken to hospital the previous evening. It was only ten in the morning when the phone rang. 'Miss Storm? It's Harry Wentworth here. I've just heard about Lucy Ryder; how is she?'

Kate explained that things weren't too bad but that Lucy was in hospital.

'I'm sorry to hear that; I'll send some flowers. May I ask, does this affect Sean at all?'

'Well, it looks like I'll be looking after him for a while longer.'

'He's a lucky lad. Miss Storm, I phoned to say that if there's anything I can do you can call on me. I could come and spend time with him there, or what I'd really like is for him to stay here. There'd be a place for you too, of course.'

She thought rapidly. It was certainly a tempting offer, but she ought to check with Luke first. And although Sean was improving every day he still wasn't fully fit.

'We'd like that,' she said, 'but obviously I've got to talk to Luke first. Can I call you back tomorrow?'

'Looking forward to it. Give my love to Sean.' He rang off. Kate wondered if there was any need to tell Luke about the conversation; the way gossip spread round here, he probably knew about it already. She went to see how Sean was getting on with his bird book.

He was an attractive little lad, but solemn beyond his years. The wispy hair now growing on his scalp made him look older than when he had been completely bald. Kate thought that she could see something of his father in him, in the intentness with which he bent his head over his work.

Although his face was still unformed he had the same bone structure as Luke; with maturity should come a rare handsomeness. If he lives that long, came the unbidden thought, and she struggled to contain the sudden pain. From his mother he'd inherited the piercing blue eyes. Kate hoped that he hadn't inherited much of his mother's character.

Eventually Sean looked up from his drawing. 'Are we going to see Grandma some time?' he asked. 'I'd like to visit her.'

'She's still quite weak,' Kate said carefully. 'We don't want to overtire her. Perhaps in a day or two.' After discussing it with Luke, Kate had decided to tell Sean that his grandmother was actually quite ill. He had taken the news with his customary stoicism, but she could tell that underneath he was quite upset. He was too young to have to suffer all this!

'What are her chances of recovery? Are they better than mine?'

She had never quite known how to answer questions like this. There were quite well-known success rates for various cancers, but she never found it helpful to know that eighty per cent of acute lymphoblastic leukaemia sufferers would survive, but the figure for children with brain tumours was only fifty per cent. However, she also didn't believe in lying to her patients.

'You're two quite different cases,' she said. 'Grandma had a heart attack; she should be all right now she's safe in hospital.'

Sean thought about this a moment and then asked, 'When can we go and look for that owl again?' Kate sighed with relief.

Luke was now making an effort to come home at least once every twenty-four hours. Sometimes it was more convenient for him to make a quick visit in the afternoon. Kate got an odd thrill when he turned up unexpectedly; it was a tiny bonus. The three of them would have a companionable drink together.

'We can cope, you know,' she told Luke as they sat with him in the conservatory. 'It'll do no one any good if you have a nervous breakdown. The thought of three generations of the Ryder family all being ill at the same time is more than I can bear.'

'And I thought I was needed and wanted,' he mocked gently. 'It's very bad for my self-esteem when you say you can manage without me.'

'There's nothing wrong with your self-esteem either. How's the American trip progressing?'

'It's coming together. At long last I think I can see some end to the work in hospital. Then I'll go on holiday.'

'That'll be the day. A bucket and spade and a train ticket to Blackpool.'

'I'll bring you back a stick of rock and a hat with "Kiss me quick" on it.'

'Chance would be a fine thing.' They both laughed.

His face changes when he laughs, she thought. Too much of the time he's serious. There's another side to his character and I hardly ever see it. It's a pity.

Perhaps he caught some part of what she was thinking, for his face became serious. 'You're supposed to be a nurse, Kate. I don't think it's any part of your job to cook and clean as well as look after Sean. Would you like me to get someone in from the village to help you?'

'No!' she said vehemently. 'Please believe me when I say that I'm quite happy with things as they are.'

'As you wish. However. . .' he took banknotes from his pocket '. . .you will have housekeeping expenses. You'd better take this.'

'Very well,' she said, taking the money. 'And I'll—'

'And, what's more,' he broke in, 'don't bother me with accounts or anything like that. Just say when you want some more.'

'Yes, master,' she said.

He shook his head. 'You just can't get the staff these days.' They laughed again.

'I phoned Mike Hamilton this morning,' he said after a pause, 'and he spoke to the hospital manager. They've arranged it all between them. From Sunday week you're on unpaid leave from the hospital. Your position is safeguarded for when you want it back. There're a few papers to sign, but it shouldn't take long.'

There seemed an air of finality about it, and once again she wondered if she was doing the right thing. Then she decided that she'd made her mind up so she'd stick to it.

'I'll have to go over for half a day,' she said. 'There are some more things I want, and I suppose I'd better give up my room.'

102   DR RYDER AND SON

'Tomorrow afternoon? I can arrange to look after Sean.' So it was decided. The decision made, she thought about something else.

She couldn't explain her feelings as she drove into the familiar, grimy courtyard of her old hospital. She didn't feel at home. Perhaps it was the thrill of memory. So much had happened to her recently that this was no longer the place where she worked, the centre of her life. It gave her a curiously naked sensation, as if she were alone in the world.

It didn't take her long to pack or store her belongings; the paperwork was quickly dealt with and then there was just time to see a few old friends. Unfortunately Mike Hamilton was at a neighbouring hospital, but she had a long chat with Denise Cowley.

'That gorgeous man you were sitting with at my party?' Denise asked with disbelief. 'If I wasn't married I'd offer to work for him for nothing.'

'It's not like that,' Kate said awkwardly. 'He's got other things on his mind. I'm nursing his son—he's got A.L.L.—relapsed once.'

'That's tough,' Denise said sympathetically, 'but remember there's always hope.'

'I know. Sean's a nice little lad and I'm fond of him.'

'I wasn't talking about Sean,' Denise said meaningfully, and Kate blushed.

It had been overcast all day and as her car climbed up the slopes of the Pennines the first few drops of rain slapped against the windscreen. After five minutes the sky darkened and the rain sluiced down. She slowed, and switched on her headlights. As she drove higher the wind increased in strength and she could feel the car being pushed about the road. By the time she reached the motorway café high on the moors she was in a full-scale storm.

She stopped, dashed to fetch a plastic cup of coffee

and decided to drink it in her car. The rain hissed across the parking area and her car rocked as the wind buffeted it.

Kate loved it, was exhilarated by the fight of the elements. It made her think of the turmoil of emotions that she was heading for. And she would fight too. Luke might think that decisions about the two of them could be made solely by him. She'd show him that this was wrong!

The storm had abated when she reached Yannthorpe and her meeting with Luke was brief. He had work piling up at hospital and he wanted to return at once.

'I've been organising,' he announced before he left. 'Tomorrow afternoon Harry Wentworth is coming round to sit with Sean for a couple of hours. Why don't you come into hospital and visit Lucy? She's been asking after you.'

Kate smiled. It was nice to be wanted. 'I'd love to,' she said. 'Er—are you happy with Harry coming?'

'Perfectly. Besides which, it benefits Sean, and, as you know, I'll do anything to get my own way.'

'You're evil,' she said. 'Has Sean been all right?'

'He's improving by the day—which, of course, is what you'd expect. I've been showing him where I'm going next month.' One brief smile and Luke was gone.

She found Sean poring over the maps and pamphlets that Luke had left. 'Look, Kate,' he said, 'a picture of a bald-eagle in Yosemite valley. Yosemite's only about a hundred miles from where Dad's going but he says he'll be too busy to visit. I'd hate to be that busy.'

'So would I,' said Kate.

Lucy was sitting up in her bed in the side-ward. Kate passed the equipment she knew so well—the cardiac monitor with its ever-passing green dot, the IV drip to break any clots in the blood.

Lucy looked comfortable. 'I feel such a fool,' she said

104 DR RYDER AND SON

as Kate sat beside her. 'I'm never ill and I've not been in hospital since Luke was born.'

'I'm sure you'll be out in a week or two.' Kate smiled. 'Look, Sean's sent you a card.'

'How is he?' The question was anxious.

Carefully Kate said, 'He's missing you but when I left him he was very well. Harry Wentworth had just arrived and they were debating whether they could put horses in Sean's bird book.'

'I miss him. I know everything possible is being done, but I've only got one child and he's only got Sean. The doctor here says I brought this attack on myself by worrying.'

'I know it's no good telling you not to worry,' Kate said gently, 'but you must try.'

'I'll do what I can.' After a pause Lucy went on, 'Luke says you saved my life.'

Kate shrugged. 'I'm sure the paramedics did more than I did.'

Lucy didn't answer for a moment. Then she said, 'I always wanted a daughter, you know——that is, as well as Luke. And if I had, I'd have liked one like you.'

Tears trickled down Lucy's cheeks as Kate leaned over to grip her hand. 'I think that's the nicest thing anyone's ever said to me.'

'This party looks decidedly gloomy!'

Kate jerked. All her attention had been on Lucy; she'd cut out the sounds of the ward around her. And somehow Luke had arrived and was leaning over them. He was dressed for work, in his white coat. She told herself that it was the shock of his arrival that made her pulse accelerate.

'I'll leave you two alone,' she said, preparing to rise. Both mother and son stretched out hands to her.

'You'll do no such thing,' Luke said. 'You're a member of the family too.' So she sat again and watched the tender way Luke kissed his mother and held her hand. She found herself wishing that he would look

GILL SANDERSON

after her in the same way, instead of manipulating her. Admittedly, his aims were unselfish—but she was still being manipulated.

The three of them chatted a little longer and then Kate and Luke saw that Lucy's eyelids were drooping, and knew that they were tiring her. Both kissed her goodbye and left.

'Have you time for a coffee before you go back?' Luke asked. 'I haven't had a break myself today.'

'I'd love one.'

He took her to the doctors' lounge again. She could tell by the quizzical way he was looking at her that he was remembering the argument they'd had the last time she was there, but he didn't say anything. Instead he fetched two coffees, pulled up two chairs so that they could face the long view up to the hills, and collapsed with a sigh.

'Just for five minutes we'll relax and look at the view,' he said. 'I feel it a constant. . .' There was the gentle but insistent sound of his bleeper.

He pulled it from his pocket and stared at the number on the little screen. She watched the expressions chase across his face—annoyance, curiosity, resignation. 'I thought I'd cleared the decks for half an hour,' he complained.

Kate listened unashamedly as he phoned. He appeared to be talking to the house officer on one of his wards. 'I wasn't expecting her till tomorrow,' she heard. 'Yes, as soon as possible. . . No, don't try to insist, but it's not you she's objecting to. . . You were quite right to call me; tell her I'll be right over.'

Kate heard the phone being replaced. Quite a few of the doctors she knew, even the good ones, would have been irritated, even angry. Luke wasn't. He sat beside her, a reflective expression on his face.

'More work?' she questioned.

'Always more work,' he acknowledged. 'It's Clare Hall—a girl I've built up a bit of a relationship with.

106 DR RYDER AND SON

She had rather an unusual cervical sarcoma. We treated it but now her GP thinks there might have been a relapse.'

'A bit of a relationship?' Kate queried.

He looked slightly uncomfortable. 'I know, Kate, they're all patients and you shouldn't get too emotionally involved with them—it can lead to bad medicine. But I've got a soft spot for Clare. Ultimately she wanted children. Now she'll never have them. I'm not perfect, you know.'

'I never thought you'd admit it,' she said drily.

'It's a definite strain.' He grinned. Then he became serious again. 'Poor Clare had everything—first a hysterectomy, then radiation and chemotherapy. It was a desperately trying time for her but she never stopped smiling.'

'And now she's relapsed?' Kate asked sadly.

'I don't yet know. My instincts say no, but we've got to check. I think Clare had just allowed herself to hope and then this happened.'

Something suddenly registered with Kate. 'You've just had a call to the ward,' she said slowly, 'and yet you're taking time to chat to me. I like it, but I'm getting to know you, Luke Ryder. You've got something in mind. What is it?'

For perhaps the first time she saw him look thoroughly uncomfortable. 'You're too shrewd,' he said. 'I hadn't even realised what I was doing myself. But I will be honest. I'm going to examine Clare—I want to try to feel the node to see if it's enlarged. If it is diseased there's an unmistakable feel to it. But, as you know, trying to palpate there in the centre of the body is intrusive and very unpleasant for the patient. I shall need to use two hands. But it's necessary. So I want you to act as my nurse and try to keep Clare calm during the examination.'

'Why me?' Kate asked, astonished.

'Because I think you are an excellent nurse who has all the qualities necessary to see that my patient suffers

GILL SANDERSON 107

as little as possible. Get her to talk about something. She's very interested in Robert Herrick. He's a poet.'

'But what about the nurses on the ward? Can't they do it? Won't they be upset?'

'They certainly could do it. But they're short-handed at the moment, and help is always pleasant.'

'Well, I'll do it if you want,' she said, 'but I want to speak to the sister first.'

In fact the sister in charge was perfectly happy to let Kate on Ebony Ward, since Dr Ryder was vouching for her. She winked at Kate and said, 'He thinks rules are made to be bent—but we love him all the same. Here, you can borrow this white coat.' Then Kate was led to the little side-ward where Clare Hall was lying. Luke was outside, talking to a serious-faced, much younger doctor.

'Don't worry, John,' Kate heard him say, 'you were absolutely right to phone me.' Then the young doctor was gone and Luke motioned her to enter the ward.

Clare Hall lay in the single bed, her dark-shadowed eyes in her white face following Luke's every movement. She was a pretty girl—but there were fine lines of worry etched round her mouth. 'Clare, this is Kate Storm.' Luke smiled. 'She's come to talk to you.'

Kate was surprised at the next five minutes. She knew just how busy Luke was, but he acted as if he had all the time in the world. Carefully drawing her into the conversation, he asked Clare about her schoolwork, her plans for university, how her father's garden was progressing. The tense figure on the bed slowly seemed to unwind.

'Right, Clare,' he said eventually, 'we'd better get started. Now, I know it's hard but I want you to keep as relaxed as you can. I've brought Kate here to talk to you. Just try to ignore me and it'll be over as quickly as I can manage.'

'I'm glad you're doing it, Dr Ryder.' Clare tried to

DR RYDER AND SON

sound calm but Kate could detect the fear and anxiety in her voice.

She pulled her chair closer to Clare's bedside. 'Dr Ryder says you're studying a poet called Herrick. I think I remember him from school.'

Clare forced a smile as she quoted, ' "Gather ye rose-buds while ye may, Old Time is still a-flying." There's a whole set of poems about making the most of life while you're living it. They're called *carpe diem* poems. It means seize the day—make the most of what you can while you can.'

Kate felt rather than saw Luke's look of approval. If she could keep Clare's attention then the examination would be so much less traumatic for her.

'So you're trying to make the most of your life?' she asked. 'What's your ambition at the moment? A levels?'

'Excuse me, Clare,' Luke put in, 'but could you turn on your side now? Just look at Kate—hold her hands if you like, and try to relax.'

Clare turned as she was asked and took Kate's proffered hands. 'These days,' she said, biting her lip, 'I suppose every new morning is a bonus. It's funny how. . .how much more you appreciate things when you think there's a chance you might soon not have them any more.'

'I can imagine,' Kate said, wondering desperately what she could say to occupy Clare's mind. 'But you're still planning ahead, still thinking about your exams?'

'Ow! Well, yes. I keep on working. If anything it's my boyfriend who stops me. He's going to Cambridge next September, and he's supposed to be working like mad. But we still spend a lot of time together. Have you got. . .a man in your life, Kate?'

'I seem to be too busy,' Kate muttered.

For the next two minutes Clare said little. Her eyes were tight shut and her grasp on Kate's hands was almost painful. Somehow Kate managed to maintain a flow of inconsequential chatter and was pleased to think that

GILL SANDERSON

perhaps she did help. Then Luke pulled the bedsheet over Clare and said in a gentle voice, 'That's it, Clare; all over now. You can relax; try to get some sleep.'

Clare sighed.

'I'll be in tomorrow to see you again,' Luke went on, 'but don't worry too much.'

'I'll try not to.'

Minutes later Kate and Luke were leaving the main ward.

'You were good with her,' Luke said abruptly. 'I'm not surprised; I knew you would be.'

'She seems a nice girl,' Kate answered. 'It was easy to relate to her. I could see a lot of myself in her.'

'Yes. I think I could too.'

She didn't know what to say to this. Instead she went on, 'What was the result of your examination? Could you feel the node?'

He nodded. 'Yes. And I'm ninety-nine per cent sure that there's nothing to worry about.'

Kate stopped and looked at him in amazement. 'Ninety-nine per cent certain? Why didn't you tell her?'

'Because I'm not a hundred per cent certain. I'll arrange with our gynaecologist for a colposcopy. Then I'll be certain.' After a moment he continued, 'There's been too much misdiagnosis of cancer, Kate. You've got to be sure.'

'I suppose so.'

They paced in silence for a while and then he said, 'The last two minutes of the examination were the most painful, the most distressing to her.'

'Yes,' she acknowledged. 'The rest was fine.'

'I'd already palpated the node and felt sure all was well. I just wanted to be certain I'd not missed anything.'

'You put Clare through that just to be certain?'

'I did. And if it had cost her twice as much pain I would have done the same.'

'Would all oncologists have treated her like that?'

He shook his head. 'Probably not. And their view

DR RYDER AND SON

could well be right. But I'm going to do what I think best.'

She didn't reply for a minute so he turned to her and said in a gentle voice, 'Doctors have to decide, Kate. It's the hardest part of the job.'

'I guess so,' she agreed.

They said goodbye at the hospital entrance after making arrangements for his next visit home. She took the now well-known road from the hospital to Yannthorpe, enjoying the changing vistas of woods and fields.

As ever when she'd spent some time with Luke there was something to think about. First she considered his grim determination to do what he thought was right. Well, that certainly was nothing new. Then she found herself thinking about Clare. The girl's fortitude had appealed to her.

She thought about what Clare had said. *Carpe diem*— seize the day. Make the most of what you have while you can. You never know how much you appreciate things until you know there's a chance you might not have them for much longer. Clare was a young girl but her illness had made her wise; Kate wondered if she could learn from her.

She was driving through a large village which had a newsagent's with a bookshop attached. On impulse she stopped, went inside and bought a paperback selection of poems by Herrick. Back in her car she quickly leafed through and found the poem that Clare had quoted. Its title was 'To the Virgins, to Make Much of Time'. Well, I am a virgin, she thought, then felt slightly warm. She read the poem then drove on.

It was obvious from the poem that when Herrick had written 'virgins' he'd merely meant young girls. But Kate found herself wondering. She *was* still a virgin— why? From gossip among friends she knew that she was unusual. She had had boyfriends, but none of them so far had really tempted her. What about Luke? The thought flashed unbidden across her mind and even though she was alone her face burned scarlet. She decided to think of something else.

Sean and Harry Wentworth had enjoyed themselves together; it gave Kate pleasure to see the happiness in both their faces. But she thought Sean might be getting overtired so she sent him to bed while she had a five-minute chat with Harry.

He made her promise to visit the stud as soon as she felt that Sean was up to it. Then he drove away, leaving her feeling slightly lost.

Sean had scattered pamphlets round the conservatory. She sat for a while looking at photographs of the Golden Gate Bridge in San Francisco, the waterfront and the cliffs of Yosemite. It all seemed so foreign, so exciting. She wondered if Sean would ever get to California and perhaps see a bald-eagle. As she looked the words of Clare Hall crept into her mind. Seize the day. It was a good motto.

Luke phoned later to say that he'd be home but he'd be late. 'Should I say that there's no need for you to wait up?' he asked. 'It's been pointless before.'

'I'll see you for supper.'

When he arrived they sat again companionably at the kitchen table. In the middle of it she had piled the pamphlets from America.

'Are all your arrangements made?' she asked, indicating the photographs.

'Well, I've practically cleared my desk. There should be nothing to stop me taking the fortnight off.'

'Could you take Sean and me with you?' She asked the question baldly, without any of the arguments she had rehearsed.

It was typical of him that he didn't reply at once. She watched his impassive face, knowing that he was considering what she had asked, knowing that he'd be well aware of all the arguments she could put forward.

112   DR RYDER AND SON

Then her heart lurched as a smile creased his face.

'I ought to say, Why didn't I think of that? We'll have to check with Marion, of course, but I think it's a great idea. Kate, you're a genius.'

He reached forward and kissed her cheek in a rare demonstration of affection. Her heart lurched again. She was glad of the affection. But she wanted much, much more.

CHAPTER SEVEN

AFTER that things happened fast—so fast that Kate didn't think of the wisdom of spending more time with Luke, and the certain attendant pain. There was so much to do.

'Marion thinks going to America is a great idea,' Luke reported on the telephone the next morning. 'Just so long as we remember not to overtire Sean. She says we still don't know exactly how much the brain can affect the body. If Sean is happy and interested, it can only improve his chances of recovery.'

'Do you agree with her?' Kate asked curiously.

'Hmm,' she heard through the receiver. His face flashed in front of her. She knew exactly how he looked when there was some difficult or interesting point to be thought about. There'd be two deep creases between his eyes, and he'd rub his bottom lip with his finger. It was a gesture that made her. . .

'I'm really not sure, Kate. I'd like to think so. Anyway, should he relapse the hospitals there are excellent.'

'Don't think that way! You've got to be positive!'

'Positive as opposed to realistic?' She heard him chuckle. 'A difficult choice to make.'

'There's no choice involved,' she told him firmly. 'You can easily be both. Think of a glass of wine when you've drunk half of it. It's now half-empty. But it's also half-full.'

'Philosophy at this hour of the morning,' he groaned. 'What have I done to deserve it? Now, I've had another word with the cardiologist and he's very pleased with Lucy's progress. He sees no reason whatsoever why we shouldn't leave her behind for a while. Says it will give her a rest. I've been in touch with Lucy's sister and she

113

can't wait to come over for a few days. Harry Wentworth will keep an eye on them and the house.'

'I'm glad about that,' Kate said. 'I was worrying about her last night.'

'I saw her this morning and she thinks it's a great idea. She really does; she's not just being unselfish. Now, you've sent for a passport; I'm having Sean put on mine. I've booked tickets for the eleven o'clock flight out of Manchester and Hugh Stenson has offered us a place for a fortnight. Everything seems to be going smoothly.'

Kate swallowed. Sometimes Luke reminded her of an avalanche. Once started there was no stopping him; any obstacle seemed to get swept away. Then she caught at something he'd said. 'Did you say Hugh Stenson?'

'Yes. He's organising the conference; I've known him for years.'

'I know him too. He spent a year in Manchester; he helped look after my father. I thought he was a very caring doctor.'

'He is.' Luke's voice was a touch too casual. 'How well did you know him?'

'Not well. He was very supportive when it was obvious my father couldn't—wasn't going to survive. We had dinner once, I think, and we exchange Christmas cards. It'll be nice to see him again.'

'I'm sure he'll be pleased to see you.' There it was again, that tiny note of disapproval. Still, she had other things to think about.

'Luke, the flight tickets. I'll pay for my own. It was my idea so I can't expect you to pay for—'

'Kate, don't be silly. Sean couldn't take this trip without you; of course I'll pay for your ticket.' She could hear the laughter in his voice as he went on, 'You're not going on holiday, you know.'

'All right,' she said, 'but I don't like feeling that I'm taking advantage of you.'

'If anyone's taking advantage, then I am. You know

GILL SANDERSON

that.' There was a pause and then he continued, 'I can't make it home tonight but I should see you some time tomorrow afternoon.'

'We'll see you then,' she managed to say evenly, and rang off. 'If anyone's taking advantage, then I am.' Yes, she did know that. And his scrupulous honesty about what he was doing only made things worse. Most of the time she could control her feelings for Luke. Occasionally, like now, they broke through. She sighed and went to find Sean.

Luke had brought two big, beautifully illustrated guides to San Francisco and California, and Sean was spending much of his time deciding what he wanted to see and do. Kate encouraged his enthusiasm, only reminding him gently from time to time that they couldn't do everything. As she watched him eagerly making lists she knew that Marion was right. A cure for any illness was as much in the brain as in the body.

'The San Francisco 49ers play at Candlestick Park,' Sean announced. 'D'you think I could get one of their baseball caps?'

'Probably a good idea,' Kate said.

'I'll take my Manchester United cap for the flight. What else should I wear?'

'We'll go to decide now. Bring your list with you.' Unlike many nine-year-old boys, Sean wanted clothes for every eventuality. Kate only managed to persuade him to leave things at home by suggesting that they might buy clothes in America.

It wasn't a holiday; Kate kept on telling herself that. But it was further than she'd ever been before, so she felt entitled to splash out a little. She managed to get into York and bought herself a new bathing costume and a glorious blue mid-length silk skirt. It could be worn for an evening dinner or dance, but because of its fullness would not be out of place in the afternoon. It looked so well on her that she had to buy three tops to go with

116　　DR RYDER AND SON

it—one matching, two contrasting. You little spendaholic, she thought.

The next fortnight was so busy, passed so quickly that she almost got used to Luke's intermittent presence. He's just an employer who is also a friend, she tried telling herself. You're a liar, her more honest side replied.

Then it was the night before the flight and Luke came late to spend the night at home. He surveyed the spotless house, the two neatly packed cases in the front hall, the light supper that Kate had prepared for him. She watched him shake his head disbelievingly. 'You're supposed to be Sean's nurse, Kate,' he sighed.

'When I want to complain I will,' she told him. 'Don't think of me as a poor put-upon skivvy who can't fight back if she needs to.'

'As if I would,' he muttered. 'I'd be too frightened to.'

She knew that he was tired. By the way he slumped into his chair in the kitchen she guessed that he'd put in more than a full day. Gently she said, 'I've done you a cheese salad and there are rolls warming in the oven. Would you like a hot drink or should I fetch you some wine?'

He scowled at her. 'I'll fetch the wine. There are some things that only a man can do.'

'Yes, I know,' she said pertly. 'I learned about them in school.'

'Wit at this hour of night,' he groaned, and went to fetch a bottle.

After the meal he looked distinctly better. 'My blood sugar was down,' he announced. 'Every doctor on the wards should carry a bar of chocolate with him. My first professor told me that.'

'So do you?' she asked.

'Well, no,' he answered sheepishly. 'It's always easier to give good advice than to take it.'

'That's a typical doctor speaking.'

He didn't answer, merely lifting an eyebrow in mock disdain.

There were a few more moments of amiable silence and then he reached inside his jacket pocket and offered her a letter. 'I discharged Clare Hall today,' he said. 'All the tests have proved negative, as far as we can see she's out of danger. She asked me to give you this note.'

Kate took it curiously. 'I can see why you liked her,' she said, tearing the envelope.

It was a short letter.

Dear Kate Storm,

Just a brief note to thank you for your care and concern ten days ago. Perhaps it was silly of me to make such a fuss over what is just a normal investigation, but your presence made it so much easier to bear. I know it's your job to look after awkward patients, but I felt you gave so much more of yourself than was absolutely necessary. Thanks again.

Dr Ryder tells me that you are accompanying him and his son to America for a fortnight. I know you're going to work, but I hope you see and do something new. Seize the day!

If you're ever in hospital when I come for a check-up, I'd very much like to have a chat.
Sincerely, Clare Hall.

Silently Kate passed the note to Luke. He read it without expression then handed it back. 'For one so young she's a wise girl,' he said. 'We get pleasure from all remission—but complete remission for Clare would give me greater pleasure than most.'

'I'll write back from America,' Kate said. 'And I would like to see her again. I think I've learned something from her.'

'What especially?' he asked with curiosity.

'*Carpe diem*. Seize the day.'

118 DR RYDER AND SON

Next morning they were off. Harry had asked if they'd like him to drive them to the airport and Luke had jumped at the offer. Sean wanted to sit in the front with his grandfather, so Kate shared the capacious back seat with Luke. Ten minutes after they started, Luke's eyes closed and he leaned back against the cushions. He had a knack that Kate had noticed in a lot of doctors—the ability to sleep whenever there was a chance. She knew that he hadn't slept much recently.

Surreptitiously she studied him. His face changed when he was asleep. The bleak lines that made him seem so formidable when he was awake and alert somehow softened. His mouth relaxed into a half-smile and his lips looked fuller, and more sensual.

The car accelerated into a bend leading to the motorway and his hand fell from his lap and landed on top of hers. For a few sweet moments she let it stay there, then sighed, and tried to ease her hand away. The large hand on hers felt the movement and its grip tightened.

He's asleep, she thought; he doesn't know what he's doing. And with the softest of pressures she squeezed back.

The queue to check their bags at the airport was short and so they were in plenty of time. Harry took Sean to look at the planes taking off and landing, and Luke took Kate for a coffee. They watched the two walk hand in hand towards the best vantage point.

'I do like Harry,' Kate said, 'and he obviously dotes on Sean. How do you get on with him now?'

'He makes me feel slightly ashamed,' Luke admitted. 'We always did get on well. But after the breakup with Maria I would never have re-established communications with him, even though I should have guessed that he'd want to. That was all your doing, Kate, and I'm grateful.'

'You didn't get on with Harry's wife, then?' Kate

GILL SANDERSON 119

probed delicately. She dearly wanted to know even though she knew that she shouldn't pry.

'Molly? She disapproved of me as a child. Not good enough for her daughter. Possibly that's one reason why Maria married me. However, I grew in Molly's estimation as I rose up the medical ladder. She'd fully accepted me just when Maria decided to turn me in.'

Kate listened hard for bitterness in his voice; she couldn't detect it. He seemed to have come to terms with his wife's behaviour. She felt happy for him.

'And what did Harry feel when you parted from Maria?' she pushed further.

This time his smile was ironic. 'He acted perfectly properly and sided with his wife and child. I couldn't disapprove. Loyalty is a great virtue, Kate.'

'If you say so,' she said. She felt a growing disbelief almost in the very existence of Maria Wentworth. How *could* anyone desert a man like Luke Ryder?

The next shock was when they went into the final departure lounge. The three of them were to travel club class. 'I didn't expect this,' she gasped. 'I would have been perfectly all right in tourist class. This must be costing you a fortune.'

'I want you with us; you're family too,' was the calm reply. 'And if it costs a fortune then it's well spent.'

'Well, I've read about club class. Just an ordinary seat would have done me. Did you know I've never been on an aeroplane before?'

'Never? What, not even to Benidorm or somewhere?'

'No. When I got to the Benidorm-visiting age my father was too ill for me to go. So somehow I seem to have missed out on air travel. But I'm really looking forward to it now.'

He put his arm round her shoulders and squeezed. 'I'm used to it. But I can remember my first flight. It was magic.'

Everyone else in club class seemed to be a veteran traveller. Kate and Sean looked on disbelievingly as their

120 DR RYDER AND SON

companions opened newspapers or settled back to doze. Didn't they know what an adventure this was? Even Luke took out a medical journal and started making notes.

There was the long taxi onto the runway, the climbing scream of the engines, the lurch forward and the bumpy acceleration, then the leap into the air, and cars, houses, planes below suddenly seemed like models placed on a vast green blanket. Kate and Sean turned to each other and grinned.

'I'm enjoying this,' Sean said.

When they reached their cruising height and speed and could take off their seat belts, Kate whispered to one of the stewardesses. Five minutes later she returned and invited Sean to come to visit the flight-deck. He returned a quarter of an hour later, enthralled. 'I want to be an airline pilot,' he announced. 'There's a great view from the front.'

Luke looked up from his journal, his eyes flicking from Sean to Kate. As so often, his expression was unfathomable. She wondered what he was thinking—and decided to ask.

'You're thoughtful,' she said.

'True. I was just thinking what a wonderful mother you would be.'

She gulped. Luke's occasional stark honesty was something that she had not yet got used to. 'Thank you,' she mumbled.

Marion had suggested that they wait until they'd had breakfast and then give Sean a sleeping pill. It wasn't to be a regular thing, but these were exceptional circumstances. After the most civilised breakfast that Kate had ever had—fresh orange juice with champagne!—she gave Sean the pill, pulled down his blind and tucked a blanket round him. He tried for a while to stay awake, but soon his eyes closed. Kate watched him for a bit, then turned to see Luke watching her.

'Enjoying the flight?' he asked her.

She grinned. 'I'm as excited as a teenager. Look at those clouds! I don't think I've ever seen anything so beautiful.'

'You know, I was coming on this flight on my own. I'm enjoying it an awful lot more with company.'

'It's nice to have your son with you.'

'I wasn't only referring to my son.'

They stared at each other in silent accord for a moment. Then a stewardess asked them if they would like a drink.

The twelve hours in the air passed quickly for Kate. There was constant attention from the stewardesses— but she never ate or drank too much. More important were the glimpses of a different life below. She saw icebergs—tiny chips of white in an infinite blue sea. Then there were the vast plains and mountains of America. She pointed out things to Luke, who smiled, infected by her enthusiasm. Then there came the different blue of the Pacific, a glimpse of the Golden Gate Bridge, and the roaring landing, nearly as exciting as take-off.

She had been a little worried as to how the flight would affect Sean, but when he woke he seemed perfectly happy and as excited as any nine-year-old would be. They moved easily through Customs and Immigration and then Luke was striding ahead to shake the outstretched hand of Hugh Stenson.

'Luke! It's good to see you!'

Hugh hadn't noticed her yet. He'd now put both his arms round Luke and was hugging him. Kate smiled to herself; she guessed that being hugged by another man was not something that Luke would really care for. But in no way did he show this.

She remembered Hugh with affection, and he hadn't changed. He was slightly shorter than Luke, but with the same width of shoulder, so he appeared stocky in build. As ever, he was wearing his grey cowboy hat.

122 DR RYDER AND SON

She recollected him one Christmas wearing it on the ward, incongruous with his white coat.

'This is Sean, my son. And I gather you know Kate Storm.'

Hugh saw her for the first time, pleasure and incredulity in his eyes. 'Kate! I don't believe it! You're even more beautiful than you were before. Give me a big, big, big kiss.'

Laughing, Kate submitted to his embrace and kissed him fondly. Over his shoulder she saw Luke looking at them disapprovingly. He's jealous, she thought happily. Then she dismissed the idea; he only disapproved of too much hugging in public.

Hugh turned and held out his hand. 'And it's good to meet you, Sean.' One of the nice things she remembered about Hugh was that he treated everyone, child or adult, cleaner or consultant, with equal courtesy.

'Luke, I might have guessed that you'd hitch up with the best-looking nurse in the north of England.'

Luke smiled, a little sourly. 'I think you've got the wrong idea, Hugh. Kate is here purely as Sean's nurse. We're friends but there's nothing—else between us.'

'I see,' said Hugh. 'Stand back and watch the rush.'

He shepherded them out into what was the largest car she had ever travelled in. They swept out of the airport, and in a few minutes were careering down a ridiculously steep street. Then they crossed the fabulous Golden Gate Bridge and headed into the green country beyond.

Hugh turned to smile at her in the back seat. 'What d'you think of my home town?' he asked. 'Isn't it gorgeous?'

She looked around and said straight-faced, 'Well, it's certainly different from Manchester.'

Hugh roared with laughter—and even Luke showed a small smile.

Two days later Kate had decided that she liked the American life. She and Sean were lying on loungers by the side of an incredibly blue swimming pool. The sun was warm and she felt smart in her new white bathing costume. It was just a pity that only Sean was there to see her in it. Then she looked down dubiously. The costume was very brief. Perhaps it was as well that there was no one else around.

Her timed ten minutes were up; she rolled over onto her back. In another ten minutes she would take Sean inside to get dressed. The two of them just weren't used to this kind of sun.

Before closing her eyes she glanced round and sighed at the beauty of the scene. They were halfway up the side of a wooded hill. Other big houses were discreetly dotted among the trees. And in the distance they could see the sun sparkling on the waters of San Francisco Bay.

The pool belonged to Hugh Stenson's parents; Hugh wasn't married and still lived with them. With a slight feeling of unreality she recollected his explaining that this wasn't their main pool, it was the guest-house pool. For the next fortnight they were staying in the guest house—a redwood building roughly four times the size of the house she'd grown up in. 'You could have stayed in the big house with me,' Hugh had explained, 'but I thought you'd feel a bit freer here.' She did.

After consulting Luke, she had decided that for the first two days she and Sean would do very little. The boy was still convalescent and she didn't want to overtire him. The novelty of his surroundings had satisfied him so far, but now he was eager to see more.

'I want to go to San Francisco,' he announced to Kate later. 'We didn't come all this way just to sit by a pool.'

'We'll see what your dad says tonight,' she answered. 'I'm sure we can work something out.'

It was a weird relationship she now had with Luke: they felt almost—she felt warm at the thought—like an old married couple. He rose very early, and had flatly forbidden her to get up to be with him. After fifteen minutes Hugh called for him and the two set off for the Seddon Hospital, twenty miles away. They returned quite late at night after having had dinner at the hospital, and Hugh usually stayed and had a drink with them.

There had been so many new sights, new sensations that she hadn't had time to think about her relationship with Luke. Every time she saw him there was still the same catch in her breathing, the same slight alteration in her heartbeat. But most of the time she was too busy to think about him.

That night she sat at the table with Luke and Hugh. Sean had just gone to bed; she always kept him up to see his father. But now was the time to plan. 'We thought of going into the city tomorrow,' she said. 'What do you think about the idea?'

Luke's eyes flicked from her to Hugh. 'What d'you think, Hugh?' he asked.

'It's a great idea,' Hugh said. 'I've got a proposition about Sean for the weekend—but he ought to go to see the city.' He fumbled in his pocket and wrote out a number. 'This is a taxi firm which will take you to the landing stage in Sausalito. Take the ferry across the bay and you're in the centre of town. Enjoy!'

She turned to Luke. 'Do you trust me to take him into a strange city?'

'There's no one I'd rather take him,' Luke answered gravely. 'Just ask Hugh where to go and what to avoid. I only wish I could come with you.'

Me too, she thought, but said nothing.

'And we saw Alcatraz from the boat and Kate said no one had ever escaped from it by swimming. And we went into this Chinese restaurant and you could have anything you wanted out of all these hot trays. And I bought a Chinese fan for Grandma; Kate said she was sure she'd like it. . .'

'So you had a good time?'

'We had an ace time, Dad; I want to go again. . . And

GILL SANDERSON 125

we went on Fisherman's Wharf; that was ace, too. . .'

Sean was tiring rapidly, though he'd insisted on staying up to tell of all that he had seen. Fortunately Luke had come home a little early, this time without Hugh. But now the day was catching up on the boy. 'Teeth and bed,' Kate said. 'You'll sleep well tonight.'

'I always sleep well.' Obediently Sean went to the bathroom.

Two minutes later Luke came back into the room after putting Sean to bed. 'I think we can say that that trip was a success,' he said.

'If he enjoyed it as much as I did, then it was.'

He looked at her assessingly. 'You didn't mind trailing a nine-year-old boy round with you?'

She shook her head. 'You could ask him if he minded trailing his nurse round with him. He was so enthusiastic, it was a pleasure to be with him.'

'Hmm.' He stroked his lower lip. 'I'm giving a presentation tomorrow. But I've managed to get the afternoon off the next day. I'll come home early and take him out. And you, Kate, can spend the afternoon looking round the shops of San Francisco on your own. Go to a show in the evening.'

'But I'm here as Sean's nurse.'

'Tell me that you really don't want to go shopping and I'll believe you.'

She gave way happily. 'Well, I wouldn't want to trail you or Sean round after me. . .'

'It's decided, then.' He rubbed his hand through his hair and went on, 'I wish I could spend more time with him. There might be a chance this weekend, but Hugh's being mysterious and has told me not to make any plans. He's got something in mind.'

'Where is Hugh tonight?' she asked casually.

He shrugged. 'Hospital business. The conference is going well, but only because people like Hugh take care of all the details.' His voice sharpened slightly. 'Why? Did you particularly want to see him?'

126   DR RYDER AND SON

'Just curious,' she said tranquilly. 'He's been here every night so far.' She hesitated and then went on, 'You say it's tomorrow you're making your presentation?'

'Yes. I'll talk for about twenty minutes and then anyone who's interested can come over for a chat.' He grinned. 'Liposomal entrapped doxorubicin. And I've got free handouts; the hospital has been printing them today.'

'Could Sean come and hear you speak? With me, of course.'

He was silent for a moment, and then when he did speak his voice was cold. 'Why should Sean want to hear me speak? Don't you think he's had enough of hospitals for a while? And what interest has he in AIDS-related diseases?'

Patiently she explained. 'He's proud of you. He doesn't need to understand what you're saying, but it would make him very happy to see you talking to an obviously important group of people.'

There was silence between them. She glanced at him but knew beforehand exactly how he would be looking; his face as set as stone, giving no indication of his thoughts. 'Sean knows he has cancer. How will he feel if he hears me coldly discussing other people's chances of survival?'

'He'll cope. After all, he has done so far.'

'So, in your opinion, listening to my talk would make him proud of me, rather than scaring him silly?'

She flinched at the directness of the question. Then, 'Yes,' she said.

'All right; I'll arrange it with Hugh early tomorrow. We'll get a car to pick you up at about half past nine.'

She sighed; there was a question that she had to ask. 'Are you agreeing because of what I've said?'

'Yes,' he said simply. 'If you trust people then you have to let them make their own decisions. And I trust you with Sean.'

'Thank you,' she said. There didn't seem to be anything else to say.

The organisation next day was alarming in its efficiency. As Luke had said, a car picked them up at half past nine. They drove through wooded hills till they came to the hospital, which also doubled as a medical conference centre.

As they drew up outside the entrance hall a young man in a light grey suit stepped forward and opened the car door. 'I'm Peter Maeschalk,' he introduced himself, and pointed to the badge on his lapel which showed his name and picture. 'Mr Stenson has asked me to be your guide until he can be with you. Now, may I get you a drink or anything?'

'No, thank you,' Kate said faintly. She hadn't expected anything like this.

'I'd like a cola,' Sean chimed in. He positively *liked* the courtesy of the Americans.

They had a few minutes to wait so Peter took them to a small sitting room and went to fetch Sean's cola. He was so anxious to please that she said yes, she would like a drink, perhaps something cool. He returned with an iced tea which she found very refreshing. After that, slightly to her surprise, Peter concentrated on talking to Sean. She sat back and listened as he skilfully asked Sean about his stay in hospital in England, his interests.

Then it was time for Luke's talk so Peter conducted them to seats in the conference hall. Sean was the youngest person there. But she was pleased to notice that at least half the audience was female, quite different from the way it would have been in a similar situation in England.

It was odd to see Luke on the platform. She'd seen him in several roles, as doctor, father, friend, but had never heard him speak in public. It came as no surprise to her to realise that he was rivetingly good. He was talking about a particular line of research into the AIDS

128   DR RYDER AND SON

virus. In twenty minutes he introduced his subject, outlined previous research and indicated how the results of his experiments so far were significant but not conclusive.

The applause when he finished was more than merely polite. Hugh came onto the platform, thanked him and gave details of how Luke would be available for discussion with anyone interested.

Sitting next to Kate were two older men. She couldn't see the names on their badges but there was something about them both that suggested authority.

'I wish that fellow worked for us,' Kate heard one of them mutter to the other. 'He's smart and he talks well.'

'Let's go and see if he can do dinner next week,' his companion replied. 'We might be able to work something out.'

Kate smiled to herself. She knew that there was no way Luke could be persuaded to leave England——at least, not for a while.

Sean had also heard the low-voiced conversation. 'They want to offer Dad a job, Kate,' he whispered. 'Wouldn't it be great to live here?'

'You'd have to leave your grandma,' she reminded him gently. 'She needs you at home.' Sean agreed that this was true.

Peter now led them back to the little sitting room and explained that Hugh would be with them as soon as he could get away. Would they like yet another drink? Feeling that this was courtesy taken to excess, both declined.

It was ten minutes before Hugh burst into the room, moving with his customary speed. 'There's a queue of doctors waiting to talk to your dad,' he said to Sean with a grin. 'I think I'll have to get him to give another talk. Now, has Peter looked after you OK?'

'He's been very helpful indeed,' Kate said, noting the faint look of apprehension on Peter's face.

'Good. I've got a surprise for you, young Sean. And

perhaps one for you, Kate. Peter, d'you want to get things ready and I'll see you in ten minutes?'

'Right, sir. Ten minutes.' And Peter was gone.

Hugh led Kate and Sean away from the conference centre and into the hospital proper, pointing out places of interest. She thought of her hospital in Manchester and grimaced. If only they had the money that had been spent on this place!

After a while she saw one or two discreet signs and realised that they were moving towards something called a rehab unit. Eventually they stopped outside a door painted bright pink. 'What I thought,' Hugh said, 'was that we could leave Sean here for an hour or so while me and you had a bite of lunch.'

She looked at him, surprised, and shook her head. 'Sean is in my charge. I don't leave him anywhere.'

Hugh was unmoved by her rebuke. 'Well, let's have a look in here and perhaps Sean will have something to say.'

It was a large, airy room, gaily decorated, divided into a number of bays. She noticed the children first. There were, perhaps, twenty of them, all roughly Sean's age. Her experienced eye soon grasped what they had in common. All had had therapy.

'Hello again, Sean. If you'd like to come over here there's a girl called Rosalie who'd like to show you something.'

Kate blinked. It was Peter again—still wearing his badge, but, instead of the formal grey suit, now in a much more casual outfit of T-shirt and jeans. He looked and sounded much more confident. After one glance at Kate, Sean took his outstretched hand and was led over to one of the bays.

Kate now realised that there were as many young adults in the room as there were children. In each of the bays there was some kind of activity. She watched as Sean was led to one with a large display screen and a little girl and an older girl standing in front of it.

130   DR RYDER AND SON

'Rosalie here has been collecting pictures of the birds she's seen in Yosemite Valley,' she heard Peter say. 'Are there any that you might see in England?'

'The young people are college students,' Hugh explained quietly. 'They get credits for the work they do here with children who are in remission. We work on a one-to-one basis—one child, one student. Many of the students want to go to medical school—and this is good training.'

They moved closer to listen to Rosalie explaining to an intent Sean just which birds she'd spotted.

'There's a doctor and a nurse constantly in attendance on the group,' Hugh went on, 'but they're very seldom needed. At the moment they're planning a trip—a three-day stay in the Yosemite Valley this weekend.'

He took her arm and urged her out of the room. As she moved, Sean waved to her in an abstracted way, but turned straight back to the display of birds.

'You know what I'm going to say next?' Hugh asked when they were in the corridor.

'There's a place for Sean on the trip if he wants it?'

'You'll recommend it to Luke?'

'You're making me redundant,' she said. 'But yes, I think I will.'

The following morning found her slightly at a loss. Luke was coming home at exactly one. He was to take Sean across the bridge and then they were going to explore Fisherman's Wharf and the science museum. Sean dearly wanted a ride on one of the bell-clanging trams that rode up the incredible gradients, and Luke had promised him one.

'Do you want me to come with you?' she had asked hesitantly.

He shook his head. 'I do,' he said, 'but you're not going to. Just for once I'm going to be unselfish. I want you to have some time to yourself; you deserve it. Stay

GILL SANDERSON 131

out for the evening if you want; Sean and I will go for a meal and some kind of show.'

In fact she would rather have gone with them than had the time to herself, but she thought it better if father and son could go out alone. They spent little enough time together.

Then the phone rang. 'Kate? Hugh here. I'm busy now so straight to business. Luke tells me he's taking Sean out for the afternoon and evening. That makes you Cinderella. May I be Buttons and take you to the ball?'

'What?' she asked, feeling stupid.

She heard him laugh. 'If you're free I'd like to take you to dinner.'

It was the last thing she had expected. But why shouldn't she go? Hugh was an old friend.

'Don't say my invitation has left you completely speechless,' came a tentative voice.

She swallowed. 'Hugh, I'd love to come to dinner.'

'Great. Pick you up at half-five? Not formal, but not beachwear either.'

'I'm looking forward to it,' she said dubiously, and rang off.

Sean then had to be prepared for his trip with his father. She was touched when she saw how excited he was, and even more touched when he said that he'd prefer it if she were coming too. But her mind was made up. Then Luke arrived in a hired car, and in the excitement of leaving she completely forgot to tell him that she was going out with Hugh. Anyway, what business was it of his?

It was odd to be alone. She sat by the pool in her costume but she couldn't relax. After a while, in desperation, she dived into the pool, hoping to work out her frustrations by exercise. But the pool was designed for bathing, not serious swimming, and there was no satisfaction in swimming just three strokes and then having to turn.

132 DR RYDER AND SON

Thoroughly irritated with herself, she climbed out of the pool and went for a shower.

She knew what was wrong. While she could see Luke, even if it was only for an hour each day, while she was wrapped up in his life, she was more or less content. She could shut out the knowledge that soon she'd have to leave. But now he'd left her, even though only for an afternoon and evening, and she felt bereft.

She made a giant effort to alter her mood. She was a nurse; she was accustomed to trauma. By sheer will-power she could cheer herself up. A derisive smile twitched over her face. There was only one thing to do: she'd phone for a taxi and go into Sausalito to spend some money.

'Now you are something gorgeous to look at,' Hugh gasped. 'I knew I was taking out someone good-looking but. . . Wow!'

Kate smiled with pleasure at the compliment; it was so obviously sincere. And without wanting to feel too proud she knew that she was looking her best.

She'd wandered round the all too attractive shops in Sausalito until, in a back street, she'd found a shop called Anita's—Hairdresser and Beautician. A quick glance through the window and Anita's had passed all the little tests she set before entering a place new to her. It was tidy, well decorated, the two assistants she could see were well groomed and well dressed. She'd entered. 'I've got a date tonight,' she'd said to Anita.

Two hours later she'd emerged, so pleased with her appearance that she'd gone back to a jewellers and splurged rather more than she could afford. Then, feeling cheerfully sinful, she'd taken a taxi back.

She was wearing the blue silk skirt and her daring white top—for the first time since that epic party when she'd knocked Dr Norman down. Her hair had been cut and streaked in a way she'd never have dared to allow in England. Anita had suggested a new shade of lipstick

GILL SANDERSON

and mascara. Round her wrist was her new purchase—a dark coral bracelet which set off her tan.

'It's three years since you took me to dinner,' she said. 'And I wanted this evening to be memorable.'

'With you looking like that, every man we meet will remember you. Now I want you to get in the car, before you vanish like a mirage.'

As he handed her into the vast car again she noticed that he too had dressed with some care. His fawn linen suit was beautifully cut, and the white shirt and floral tie were both silk.

He took her to a floating restaurant moored in one of the many tiny harbours that line the banks of San Francisco Bay. From their table they could see the great arches of the Oakland Bridge and the skyscrapers of the city behind. He suggested that they have the speciality of the house—a seafood salad—and a white wine from the Napa valley, only thirty miles further north.

Hugh was an engaging companion, and throughout their delicious meal they chatted easily about old friends and the differences between English and American medical life. She felt happy, relaxed.

It was dark when they finished. They walked along the harbour wall, the great light-show that was San Francisco reflected on the dark waters beside them. He held her hand, which she didn't mind, but when he tried to slip his arm round her waist she moved away, pleasantly but firmly.

They stopped to watch the silhouette of a ship sliding by. 'This is a wonderful city, Kate,' he said. 'Are you enjoying your stay?'

'Very much. Of course, this is work, not a holiday—but I love it.'

'Would you like to work here full-time?' His voice sounded casual, but she could tell that there was an underlying tone of seriousness. He was offering her a job!

134 DR RYDER AND SON

'You mean, move to America? Leave my job in England?' she floundered.

'You'd have to wait till your job with Sean and Luke is finished, of course. But that shouldn't be long.'

He obviously recognised that the invitation had taken her completely by surprise and went on, 'Part of my job is getting the best possible staff available. After all, we pay enough. I want you on one of my wards.'

'Well, I'm flattered,' she said slowly. 'It's just that—'

'I don't want a decision. I just want you to think about it. Why don't I send you a packet of information? You can get back to me with any questions—even discuss it with Luke if you like.'

'Yes, I could discuss it with Luke.' The trouble was that she thought she knew what his advice would be. Take the job.

While she was brooding Hugh had taken hold of her other hand and gently pulled her towards him. When he leaned to kiss her she turned her cheek to him. Then she pulled him towards her, squeezed him once and then pushed him firmly away.

'Hugh, I'm sorry,' she said sincerely, 'but I just don't think of you that way. I hope we can be friends, but it would be wrong of me to let you think we could ever be lovers.'

The dark figure in front of her remained silent for a moment. Then he spread his arms wide and said, 'Well, I tried. I like you, Kate; you're honest with me. Still friends, then?'

'Of course we're friends.' Even in the dark she could see his slumped shoulders; her rejection had affected him more than she had realised. 'Come on, Hugh; walk me to the end of the pier.' She took his arm and urged him onwards.

'The offer of the job still stands, of course,' he said. 'I may be an unsuccessful lover but I am still an ace hospital administrator. Think about it, Kate.'

'I will,' she promised. They'd stopped at the end of

GILL SANDERSON 135

the little pier and she took in the magical scene in front of her—the hills, the lights, the lapping of the water below. She went on, 'It's just that—I'm not sure about my future right now.'

'I see.' They turned to move back towards his car. After a few steps in silence he asked her gently, 'Kate, are you carrying some kind of torch for Luke?'

She could have told him that it was none of his business. But she felt that his question was motivated by concern for her. 'I suppose so,' she said.

Obviously choosing his words carefully, he said, 'You must do as you think best. But he told me—that is, I think that under his present circumstances, and because of that lousy wife of his—well, I wouldn't hold out much hope.'

'I see.' Ideas, half-formed suspicions suddenly gelled in her mind. 'Did he suggest you take me out? To get me off his back?'

'Kate!' He was genuinely hurt at the suggestion. 'You know what I've always thought about you!' After a moment he added uncertainly, 'But I certainly wouldn't have invited you to dinner if I'd thought you and he had something going.'

'So he told you that there was nothing between us. And you might as well move in.'

By now Hugh was obviously upset and embarrassed. 'You're twisting things. Luke was concerned about you.'

'I'm sure he was. Just one last question, Hugh: who suggested this dinner?'

'Luke did,' Hugh muttered.

CHAPTER EIGHT

KATE was angry—so angry that she wanted to hit something—or preferably someone. But that someone wasn't Hugh. Somehow she managed to keep up a flow of casual conversation as they drove back to the house, but she could tell by Hugh's wary answers that he was not fooled.

'No, I'll not come in,' he said as he handed her out of his car. 'I've got work to do.'

'I'm sure you have,' she said ironically. She leaned forward and kissed him quickly. 'Hugh, I've enjoyed tonight. I really have. I'll think about the job and, well—sorry about the other thing.'

'Some man will be very lucky,' he replied enigmatically. 'Goodnight, Kate.' She watched the lights of his car disappear up the drive to the main house, and then turned, ready for battle.

Luke was sitting reading at the kitchen breakfast bar, a mug of tea in his hand. Just for a moment it reminded her of the occasions when they had sat together late at night in the kitchen at Yannthorpe; her heart pounded at the thought. Then she saw the note she'd left him, explaining where she'd gone. There had been no need for the note; he already knew. Her temper blazed again.

'You're back early,' he said casually. 'Did you have a good time?'

'As good a time as could be expected. Certainly I enjoyed myself more than your good friend Hugh. Did Sean enjoy his day?'

There was no mistaking the coldness of her tone. And she knew that Luke had never been someone who would back away from a fight. 'Sean and I had a wonderful

136

time. Now, is something wrong?' He seemed puzzled. 'Have I or Hugh offended you in any way?'

'Hugh hasn't. You have.'

'Well, I'm sorry. Will you tell me what it is?'

She tried to match the calmness of his tone, but it was difficult. 'I object—strongly—to being handed over to your friend just because I'm an annoyance to you.' She faltered slightly. 'You know that I am—attracted to you. You've told me clearly that there's no prospect of a relationship between us, and I've accepted that. My pain is mine alone. It is degrading that you think you can push me into the arms of your friend so that I won't become an embarrassment.'

His face whitened, but his voice remained calm. 'Kate, you could never be an embarrassment or an annoyance to me. I knew Hugh wanted to see more of you so I suggested he invite you out. I can offer you nothing. He could offer you a lot.'

'You're an insensitive lump, Luke Ryder!'

'Possibly I am. But I acted in good faith.'

'Good faith is the worst excuse there is. I like Hugh, but not as a lover. How do you think I feel when the man who's rejected me tries to fit me up with a substitute?'

There was a long pause. She could tell that he was angry—angrier than she'd ever seen him. His eyes glittered in his white face and for a moment apprehension fluttered in her breast. What had she said?

But she should have remembered his iron self-control. Eventually he said, 'Kate, I'm sorry. You mean a lot to me and Sean, and not for the world would I do anything to upset you.'

'You're a devil, Luke. Here I am, in the right, and you've made me feel in the wrong.'

'I can only say I'm sorry again.'

Looking at him, she felt her temper vanish. Telling a valiant lie, she said, 'I guess I'm sorry too. Sorry about my outburst, that is. Perhaps I'm just being foolish and feminine.'

138 DR RYDER AND SON

She had forgotten his astuteness. 'You're not, Kate. I appreciate what you're trying to do. You're trying to find an excuse for me.'

'Suddenly, Doctor, you're an expert on how I think!'

'No, Kate, I'm not an expert on anything to do with you. But the more I get to know you, the more I appreciate——' He stopped, and she knew that he was choosing his words with care. 'The more I appreciate what you're doing for Sean and me. I've hurt you; please forgive me.'

What could she say? She went to him and, for once sure of herself, kissed him—an amiable, non-sexual kiss. 'You know, there should be warnings broadcast against you: To all lonely, depressed females—storm imminent in Luke Ryder area. Avoid at all costs; possibility of emotional damage.' Seeing his bewildered face, she shouted, 'No, I am not lonely, not depressed. I was angry that you tried to pass me on to your friend. But now I have forgiven you!'

The silence lengthened. It suddenly struck her that Luke was more than her friend: he was her employer. She felt uneasy. Not quite sure what to do, she watched him put down his cup, stand, move round the table. For a moment they stood face to face and then his arms were round her. His mouth pressed on hers in a violent, demanding, even cruel kiss. For a moment she thought that she might resist, but then she swayed to him, caught up in a passion that enveloped them both.

They stood there for endless moments. Then, with infinite reluctance, he put her from him. 'You *do* know what you mean to me, don't you?' he asked in a tortured half-groan. Though their bodies were apart he still clutched her hands.

'Yes, Luke. And you mean the same to me.'

For a while they gazed at each other, the secrets stripped from their souls. Then, deliberately, he walked back and sat at the table again. He sighed. 'I guess I

GILL SANDERSON 139

deserved all the names you called me,' he said. 'Now would you like a cup of tea?'

'I think I need one. Tell me about your afternoon.'

Hugh came back with Luke the next evening and Luke explained that in principle he was in favour of Sean going on the three-day trip to Yosemite. However, he wanted her opinion.

'Sean's very keen on it,' she said. 'He very much likes Peter and the rest of the group. Quite frankly, having let him join in the planning, it would be cruel not to let him go.'

'There'll be no medical problems,' Hugh promised. 'We've got a backup team of doctors and nurses ready at ten minutes' notice.'

'Right, then,' Luke said. 'It's settled. He's reading in bed now, so I'll go and tell him he's going. He won't sleep otherwise. And thanks for the chance, Hugh. There's nothing quite like this in England.'

'My pleasure.' Hugh beamed.

There was silence between Hugh and Kate until they heard the bumps overhead, signalling that Luke was in his son's bedroom. Then Hugh said in a strained voice, 'Everything all right after last night?'

'Fine, thanks,' she reassured him. 'We had a bit of a row, but it cleared the air. And I've still got your offer of a job in mind.'

'Good, good. I wouldn't want two people I very much care for to be unhappy.'

She reached over the kitchen table to pat his hand. 'I think you're lovely, Hugh.'

'I try,' he said. 'I try. Now, here's a form that needs to be filled in about Sean's needs for the trip, and here's a detailed plan of what he'll be doing and where he'll be doing it...'

She leaned forward to look.

Obviously happy that he'd caused no friction between two of his friends, Hugh stayed chatting another half-

140 DR RYDER AND SON

hour. When he left, Kate and Luke sat still at the table. It was late, but Kate didn't want to go to bed quite yet. Neither, apparently, did Luke.

'You know, I came here to look after Sean,' she said. 'And now I'm helping send him away. You'll be thinking that I'm a slacker.'

'I certainly do,' he said with mock severity. 'There will be a corresponding reduction in your wages.'

She rolled her eyes, 'But sir, I need money for shoes.' Then she collapsed, giggling. 'Seriously, though,' she went on, 'since I'm having a three-day holiday at your expense, I think I should pay at least some towards my air fare.'

'No, Kate! We've been over this before. Now, please don't mention it again.'

'All right,' she agreed. 'I won't. Want another cup of tea?'

He nodded and she poured him one.

'Sean's away for Friday, Saturday and Sunday,' he said. 'You can get some shopping done, see some of the sights.'

'Fine,' she said airily. 'I take it that you'll be working through?'

'Hmm.' He rubbed his lower lip. 'I've got full days on both Friday and Sunday but somehow I've managed to get Saturday off.' After a pause he went on, 'Remember our day sailing?'

'Very well,' she said. 'Especially our little talk just before we got home. The rest I enjoyed.'

He winced. 'Sorry. Look, there's no reason why you should—but if you wanted to come out with me on Saturday I think I could promise you an interesting time.'

She knew that it was the last thing she ought to do. Then Clare Hall's words rose in her mind. Seize the day. 'I'd love to,' she said.

Friday she spent looking round San Francisco. Without Sean she had more time to browse in Chinatown, and she felt entitled to look through a couple of the giant stores in the city centre. Shopping was totally different from in Manchester! She bought herself two beautiful silk scarves, and a cream linen suit that looked tremendously smart.

It was strange, too, to welcome Luke back from work without Sean being around. She knew that he could feel her slight embarrassment, and this only made things worse. She'd put her new purchases away, but he spotted a luxurious carrier bag from one of the large stores. She hadn't been able to bring herself to throw it in the bin.

'What have you bought?' he asked. 'Anything specially nice?'

'Just a few clothes,' she mumbled. 'Nothing very exciting. A suit and a couple of scarves.'

'Well, go and put the suit on. I want to see it.'

She looked at him, amazed. 'You can't possibly!'

'Oh, yes, I can. First of all, I've had a hard day slogging away at the peculiar antics of the AIDS virus. It was interesting but wearing. I now want to look at something attractive, and if it's frivolous too so much the better. Secondly, when most women buy clothes and bring them home, they feel anxious and want a friend's opinion. All you've got is me. Don't you want my opinion?'

'I think you're completely mad,' she muttered, but went upstairs anyway.

If he wants a fashion show he can have it, she thought, shrugging out of her shirt and jeans. With the new cream suit she put on tights and high-heeled court shoes, ran a comb through her hair and applied a touch of lipstick. Quickly she surveyed herself in her bedroom mirror. Not bad!

The reaction to her efforts was gratifying in the extreme. 'And now we have Kate Storm,' she said in a mock-sultry voice, parading across the kitchen with one hand on her hip and the other waving an imaginary cigarette. 'Kate is wearing an ensemble in cream. A positive bargain at five thousand pounds.'

142 DR RYDER AND SON

For a moment he was speechless. Then he said, 'I know it didn't cost five thousand pounds, but on you, Kate, it looks as if it might have. You look. . .fabulous.'

'Compliments indeed! For your information, this came off the slightly reduced rack.'

'Hmm. I will now stick my neck out and say how smart I thought you looked when you'd had your hair done the other night. I didn't say so then because—' he coughed '—I didn't think the time propitious.'

'Such sensitivity!'

'Such cowardice,' he said drily.

For a while he looked at her and she could tell by his changing expression that their frivolous few minutes had passed. Something far more intense was replacing them. Just now she didn't want to know exactly what. 'If you put the kettle on I'll go and change,' she said, and made a hurried exit.

When she returned he had made the pot of tea that they normally shared at night and was studying a map. He'd obviously decided to change the mood. 'We're going here tomorrow,' he said, and pointed.

She leaned over his shoulder to look. The map was of the coast north of San Francisco and he was indicating a cove about eighty miles away. The coastline looked rocky, and there were only woods inland. 'It looks a bit wild,' she said.

'It's one of the most beautiful areas in America. And for some reason it's one of the loneliest. I know you're a good swimmer, but have you ever been diving?'

The abrupt change of topic threw her for a minute. 'You mean with a scuba-lung on my back? No, never. But I wouldn't mind trying.'

He laughed. 'Even the best swimmer needs a good few weeks' tuition in a swimming bath before it's safe to dive in the sea. No, I meant have you ever swum with a face-mask and a pair of fins?'

'No,' she said, wondering what was so marvellous about the idea.

He guessed what she was thinking. 'Don't knock it till you've tried it. You're going to have a whole new experience tomorrow. And if I know anything about you you'll love it.'

'I'm willing to try anything.' Dark eyes flashed at her. 'Of course,' she said hurriedly, 'I meant almost anything.'

'I'd like to get an early start. Up at six OK?'

'If we're going swimming, I'll do us a breakfast.'

'That might be a good idea.' He yawned hugely. 'I think I'll go to bed.'

Just before he went she asked, 'How do you feel with Sean not here?'

He looked at her curiously. 'You tell me. How d'you think I feel?'

Carefully she said, 'You miss him, but you know he's safe, in good hands and enjoying himself, so there's a slight sense of relief; you're looking forward to a day without him. And because of that you're feeling slightly guilty.'

She had no idea what he was thinking. His face took on that neutral expression she'd seen so often, that gave away nothing. She guessed that it would be a good expression to have when telling people bad—or good—news. After a moment he said, 'I think you know me better than I know myself, Kate. Goodnight.'

He went to bed. She occupied herself in the kitchen for a minute or two, but she knew that she was only wasting time. So she went to bed too. But, as she had known, she didn't sleep.

Next morning things were different. They were pals, about to enjoy a day in the open air together. It certainly wasn't all she wanted from him, but it was pretty good.

After breakfast he told her what to wear and pack— swimming costume, old, warm clothes, a big towel and a complete change. She'd already organised a pack of

144   DR RYDER AND SON

sandwiches and a big vacuum flask of coffee. Then they were off in the hired car.

She enjoyed this kind of day. Swimming, sailing, walking—it didn't matter what. They'd be in the open air and they'd be together.

For a while they drove through the wealthy suburbs of Marin County and then they were on the 101 Freeway, moving rapidly north. After half an hour Luke turned left and they dived up and down a country road, through a great forest.

'Look,' he said, and pointed to one side. There, miles from anywhere and in the middle of the thickest of woods, was a great, bulbous gold dome, with flags streaming from it.

'What on earth is it?'

He shrugged. 'Probably one of those lunatic religious sects. See, they've built a ten-foot wall—but I don't know if it's to keep people out or in.'

'And in such beautiful countryside too.'

'Wait till you see the coast.'

Soon enough they did—a rocky, wind-torn coast, with the spray from the Pacific waves visible from the road, a mile away. The road itself was strangely quiet, winding in and out but always just in sight of the sea. The few villages they passed through were tiny. Like San Francisco it was exhilarating, but in a different way.

After an hour they dropped to sea level and ran through a handful of cottages, too few to be called a village. He slowed down, obviously looking for a turn-off. Five minutes later they found it, and he turned onto a bumpy track. They bounced along for another ten minutes, through scrubby, wind-twisted trees.

'We've arrived,' he said. There were a dozen or so vans and trucks parked in a little open space. He pulled in beside them and said, 'Go and have a look.'

She walked to the edge of the clearing, looked down, and the view took her breath away. Quite a wide path ran down a steep hillside below her, leading to a cove.

GILL SANDERSON 145

From one side of the cove there was a ridge of rock running out to see, sheltering a large area of calm water.

'Hi there! Dr Ryder?' A number of people were grouped on the silver sand below, most of them in neoprene wetsuits, and one of them was waving.

'We'll be right down,' a voice behind her shouted, and there was Luke, carrying their bags.

'You didn't tell me we were going out with a group,' she said, just slightly disappointed.

'You never dive unless you've got backup. Come on; I know you're going to enjoy this.'

On the way down the path he explained that Martin Track, one of Hugh's friends, was a keen diver and had offered them the chance of coming on a club meet.

'He's brought kit along for both of us,' Luke went on. 'A suit and belt, fins and mask each. And a spare tank of air if I want to dive.'

It was all new and looked a bit dangerous to her. But then she thought, Seize the day—and decided that she would enjoy herself.

The group was friendly and helpful but obviously far more interested in their diving than in the two newcomers. Luke explained that he was a trained diver and would like to introduce Kate to snorkelling. They were promptly handed their kit and invited to get on with it.

'I don't need to tell you, do I, Doctor,' Martin asked, 'you keep beginners well inside the bay?'

'I know the dangers,' Luke acknowledged.

She changed into her costume behind a little wall. Then Luke came striding over, clad only in brief black shorts. She'd seen him stripped to the waist before and had secretly marvelled at his taut muscles, the fine lines of hair on his chest and forearms. But now there was little left to her imagination; he was practically naked! She tried hard not to look at the tight briefs.

He, however, wanted to dive. He helped her into the wetsuit, gave her fins and a mask. Then he donned his own wetsuit and led her to the sea.

146 DR RYDER AND SON

'You put your fins on at the last minute,' he advised her. 'Otherwise you have to walk like a frog.'

Wearing the wetsuit made the water seem surprisingly warm. When they were waist-deep he sat her down and showed her how to fasten the mask, and how, once she was under the water, to use her nose to blow out water that leaked inside. Then, side by side they made for deeper water. It was so easy to swim with the fins.

'Don't hyperventilate,' he told her. 'Just take a deep breath and dive. I'll be right with you.' So she did as he said. And it was like entering Wonderland.

The fins made it easy to swim down and the mask made everything clear. Hand in hand they dived to a patch of white sand and then turned and swam through a forest of gently swaying seaweed. It shocked her; she'd always thought that seaweed would lie flat on the seabed. It didn't. Eerie tendrils brushed across her and moved down her body.

It seemed ages before she felt that she needed more air. She had copied Luke, moving only slowly and thus conserving oxygen. Now they rose to the surface together.

'Well?' he asked her when their heads broke water and they dragged in their first breath.

'Luke, Luke, it's magic! I never guessed it. . . Let's go down again.'

'No problem. Remember, never get out of breath and never hyperventilate.' Down they went again. This time she was thrilled to see a shoal of tiny silver fish.

After an hour he told her that they ought to go in for a rest. 'But I'm enjoying myself!' she protested. 'And I'm not the least bit tired.'

He smiled. 'You'll be surprised,' he said. 'Let's go and have a coffee and a sandwich.'

She *was* surprised. They peeled off the wetsuits, towelled themselves roughly and sat in the sun. Luke said that he'd run up to the car and fetch the bag with

GILL SANDERSON 147

the drinks and sandwiches. So she leaned back and shut her eyes. The sun was warm on her face. . .

She slept for nearly an hour. 'But I never drop off like that,' she said, amazed when he gently shook her awake.

'Your core temperature was down. The chill gets you, even through the wetsuit. So the blood moves from your brain to try to warm your internal organs.'

'Sort of like shock?' she asked, interested.

'Physiologically, very similar. But it takes longer to take effect; that's what can make it dangerous.'

'I see.' She drank the coffee he offered her. 'And why were you so keen on my not hyperventilating?'

'Ah. That can be very dangerous. You know when you hold your breath—after a while your lungs start to burn and you feel really distressed?'

'Yes.'

'Well, it's not actually lack of oxygen that produces the feeling. It's the build-up of carbon dioxide in your bloodstream. Hyperventilating washes the carbon dioxide out of your blood temporarily. So there you are underwater, your oxygen runs out and you black out without any pain whatsoever.'

She blinked. 'Dangerous business, this diving.'

'Only if you don't know what you're doing. Now, fancy another swim?'

This time he took her further out, beyond the cove. They dived and she was entranced to find herself in another forest of weed. But this time she couldn't see the bottom and Luke wouldn't let her swim further down. 'Kelp,' he explained when they surfaced. 'Some of it grows up to two hundred feet long. From the seabed nearly to the surface.'

'Were we two hundred feet from the seabed?'

'I don't think so. Perhaps about a hundred feet.'

The thought of that depth—populated by who knew what kind of sea creatures—suddenly made her uneasy. 'I think I'd like to go in now,' she said.

For a while they sat on the beach and chatted to the

148 DR RYDER AND SON

club members there. They were made welcome and invited to stay for the evening; there was going to be barbecue. Kate was interested in finding out that they were all non-medical—not a doctor or nurse among them. It struck her that in some ways her circle of friends was a bit limited.

Then Martin came over and offered Luke something that seemed to Kate like a tyre-lever. 'Shall we look for abalone?' Martin asked.

Luke looked at her. 'Kate, I. . .'

She guessed. 'You want to go out with Martin to do something I'm not experienced enough to try. So off you go. I've had a glorious time, but I've had enough. Honestly, I need a rest now.'

'OK. Perhaps half an hour.' He strode across the sands.

Quite a few of the other divers had decided to call it a day. Kate noticed that they stripped off their wetsuits and then went for a quick dip in the sea in just their costumes. She decided to do the same herself; it was chilly but it refreshed her.

The time passed quickly. She dressed, and then chatted to the others. It seemed no time before Luke came back and presented her with two great shells about ten inches across. 'Abalone,' he said.

She looked at them dubiously. 'What do I do with them?'

'You wait and see. Another experience for you. Now I think I'll get dressed too.'

It was while he was changing that it happened. Quite a few of the group were swimming in the warm shallows, shouting amiably and splashing each other. One was further out than most. Then one of the men on the beach looked out and shouted. 'Carl—jellyfish! It's a Lion's Mane.'

Kate's head jerked up at once. The man shouting was anxious—panicking even. She watched in disbelief as

GILL SANDERSON 149

the happy group in the water hastily swam or waded ashore. What a fuss about a jellyfish!

Then she heard the man in the centre of the bay yell, and she knew why there was a fuss. There was agony in that scream. Her eyes picked him out; near him was something bright and yellow——the Lion's Mane. She ran to the edge of the sea and watched as the more daring of the group dashed back into the water and helped their friend out.

'Are you all right, Carl?' someone asked anxiously. But it was clear to Kate that he was not.

Across his chest, from waist to high by his neck, was an angry red weal. She had never seen anything like it before. The two men who had pulled Carl out of the water were now having to hold him upright; he appeared incapable of standing and was obviously in considerable pain. She noted the beginning of a discharge from his nostrils.

No one quite knew what to do. One of the group muttered, 'I know the sting hurts——but I didn't think it was this bad.'

'Carry him up the beach and lie him on the grass,' Kate said suddenly. 'One of you go and shout for Dr Ryder. This man is in trouble.'

Happy that someone had taken charge, they did as she said. She knelt by the recumbent figure. Sweat was pearling his forehead. But he'd been in the chill water not two minutes before! 'Has anyone got any kind of first-aid kit?' she asked. No one had.

Luke knelt opposite her; never had she been so pleased to see someone.

'Jellyfish sting?' he asked.

She shook her head. 'Far more than that, I think. Temperature is up. Pulse is irregular and weak.'

'Breathing troubled and getting worse,' he said grimly. 'And look——his face is cyanosed.' She saw the bluish tinge to his face that indicated that Carl wasn't getting enough oxygen.

150 DR RYDER AND SON

Luke looked up. 'You two—go and find a phone; we need an ambulance here with paramedics, quickly. Tell them it's a jellyfish sting. And the patient's gone into anaphylactic shock. Got that?' The two men nodded, and set off up the path at a run.

'You two,' Luke said to another pair, 'take a car and go to the village. Ask if there's any kind of first-aid kit. What you need is epinephrine or antihistamine. Here, I'll write the words down. There isn't much chance, but we must try everything.' Clutching the scrap of paper, the next two ran off.

'I'm not happy about his breathing,' Kate murmured to Luke.

Carl's muscular chest strained for breath but nothing came from his throat but the faintest of wheezing sounds. He was now in considerable distress. 'Can't you do anything? You're a doctor,' came a call from one of the distressed onlookers, and Kate heard a note of hysteria in the voice.

She stood and pulled the man to one side. 'Look, you're not helping. Now we need a small, sharp-bladed knife and a couple of ballpoint pens. Ask everyone. And get some towels we can use as bandages.'

Calmer now that there was something he could do, the man did as she said. Kate kneeled opposite Luke again. Between them Carl's tortured body writhed and twisted. She forced herself not to be affected by his pain. At the moment he needed her dispassionate skill and judgement.

Luke had his hands on each side of Carl's throat. 'The pharynx is nearly closed,' he said tautly. 'Soon there'll be no air getting through at all. Somehow I'm going to have to perform an emergency tracheotomy.'

'I've asked for a knife,' she said.

Suddenly two hands appeared in front of them, one holding four ballpoint pens, the other two pocket knives. Luke glanced across at her. 'You think of everything.' Then he selected a pen and took out the centre. He opened both knives and tested the blades. 'Hyperextend the neck, please, Nurse,' he said formally. She wriggled round and crouched behind Carl's head, pulling it backwards and lifting the chin.

She watched as with swift, precise movements Luke stretched the skin beneath the Adam's apple then cut sharply downwards to make an incision through the fibrous tissue of the trachea. As blood welled upwards he thrust the pen into the hole he had made.

Air whistled through the hollow pen as Luke held it in position. The silent group watched. She knew that they'd be horrified. Then the breath rushed more slowly in and out of the little pipe and the chest moved up and down in a more normal rhythm. Carl's body relaxed.

'Cyanosis is going,' she reported.

'Good. That's the first hurdle over. He's a healthy lad; we'll just have to hope his heart will hold on until the paramedics arrive. Otherwise, closed-chest heart massage.'

They waited fifteen anxious, silent minutes. She dabbed away the blood that ran from the cut that Luke had made, while he kept his hand on Carl's throat, holding the pen in position. Carl's heartbeat wasn't strong, but somehow it kept going.

Something in the back of her mind registered a distant buzzing noise, slowly growing louder. The noise suddenly increased; there was a great clatter overhead and instinctively she flinched. She looked up. A blue and white helicopter flew low over their group, circled the beach and then put down about fifty yards away. As the whirling rotors slowed two uniformed men jumped out.

'Now, that's what I call an ambulance service,' Luke said drily.

It struck her that it was the second time in less than a month that she'd had to send for paramedics. The two Americans who scrambled over wore different uniforms but had the same air of competence as the British pair.

152   DR RYDER AND SON

'Anaphylactic shock,' one of them grunted. 'And here is just the thing.'

He injected the epinephrine straight into the muscles of Carl's chest, then vigorously rubbed the site of the injection to hasten the diffusion of the drug. It worked fast. Within minutes Carl's pulse was stronger, his heartbeat more positive.

The two paramedics now turned their attention to Luke's emergency breathing gear. 'That is good,' the older of the two said with a smile. 'When I was in Nam I saw someone do the same with a drinking straw. But I think we've got a better system here.'

He tore open a bag and took out a sterile plastic tube fitted with a harness that wrapped round the neck. Carefully he eased out the pen and inserted the plastic tube.

'Things are looking better now,' he said cheerfully. 'Would a couple of you strong young men like to go and help my partner along with the stretcher?'

He turned to Luke. 'Gather you're a doctor. Good thing you were around; you saved his life.'

Luke shrugged. 'There were two of us here. He was lucky—or unlucky.'

After that there was little for Kate to do. Carl was carried to the helicopter and whisked smartly to hospital. Four of his friends followed in their cars, saying that they would get in touch with Carl's father and deal with any other problems. A police car arrived and the driver took addresses and brief statements. Then it was all over, and everyone felt a sense of anticlimax.

Martin came to speak to Luke and Kate. 'We've got to thank you two,' he said awkwardly. 'I thought I was tough, but there's no way I could have stuck a knife in a man's throat.'

'Take a first-aid course.' Luke smiled. 'You never need it until you need it desperately.'

'I'll do that. The other thing is. . .well, you were invited to our cook-out, but none of us feel like it now. OK if we call it off?'

GILL SANDERSON 153

'No problem. And thanks for the loan of the kit.'

'It was nothing. Hope to see you again soon.'

Luke put a friendly arm on Kate's shoulder. 'D'you mind going home at once?'

'No. To tell you the truth I feel tired. The first bit of the day was fantastic. I suppose the second bit was fantastic too. Lucky for Carl that you were here.'

'Lucky for Carl that *we* were here,' he corrected her gently. 'You know I couldn't have done it without you.'

Hand in hand they walked to the top of the cliff.

CHAPTER NINE

KATE slept for most of the ride home. She hadn't intended to; she'd wanted to chat to Luke to make sure that he didn't nod off at the wheel. And she'd already slept once that day. But he would have no argument. He yanked at the lever that made her seat recline and told her to close her eyes.

'Just for five minutes, then,' she told him. 'I think it's because I'm not used to the cold water.'

'Well, I am. Don't worry about me.' So she shut her eyes, and the next thing she knew they were home and he was gently shaking her awake.

Both went straight upstairs to shower. The sea water had left her feeling rather sticky, and there were blood-stains on her shirt. Instead of her customary jeans or shorts she put on a sleeveless blue dress. She just felt like being feminine. When she went back downstairs she knew that Luke had noticed and approved.

There was a message from Hugh on the answering machine. 'Give the lad some space! He's having a great time so don't bother to ring.'

'It seems like everyone can predict me,' Luke said sardonically. Then he phoned the hospital where Carl had been taken and learned that he was out of danger.

'Of course I'm pleased for him,' he said, 'but I'm also just a touch relieved. If anything had happened to him— well, I could have found myself being sued.'

'But you saved his life!'

'This is America, Kate. Suing doctors and hospitals is common.'

'It's not my idea of medicine.' She handed him the mug of tea she'd started making the minute they got home and for a moment they sat in friendly silence.

GILL SANDERSON 155

'It's still early,' he said, 'and you must be ravenous. Let's be real Americans. How about a barbecue?'

'I'd like that,' she said. 'I really would.' The house had its own built-in barbecue by the pool. Once or twice she'd lit it in the evening to grill Sean a hamburger, but she'd never cooked there with Luke.

'You've got a real treat coming—something you've never had before. Can you rustle up some bread and a salad?'

First she started the barbecue. Then she tore lettuce and cut tomatoes and watched Luke, fascinated.

He took the two giant shells that he'd dived for and prised them open. Some of the contents were thrown in the garbage can and he was left with two large lumps of greyish meat, which didn't look too appetising. To her surprise he took a lump, wrapped it in a towel, whirled it round his head and slapped it hard on the marble floor. 'This is the traditional way of doing it,' he said.

She loved watching him work. His movements were exact and coordinated and he appeared utterly absorbed in his task.

'These are a real delicacy,' he said. 'You're only allowed to take four at a time and you must dive for them without an air tank. It's the State's way of trying to preserve stocks. Here, would you like a shell?'

She looked enthralled at the shell he offered her. Outside it was rough and grey, but the inside shone with a dozen pearl-like colours—rose, silver and the deepest of greens.

'It's lovely,' she said. 'May I have it?'

'It'll smell. But I've got some pool acid we can clean it with, and I'll find some clear shellac. Then you can have a matching pair on your dressing table.'

She knew that the shells would become two of her most cherished possessions. But all she said was, 'You'd better do a couple for Sean too.'

'I certainly will. Now let's start with some wine.'

156 DR RYDER AND SON

He took the bottle from the fridge and poured them each a glass. They were now ready to carry the food outside. And just as she picked up the salad bowl her arm knocked the pepperpot; it fell and shattered.

'Darn it. That's all the pepper we've got,' she said, sweeping glass and black grains into a pan.

'You can't eat abalone without pepper. Look, I'll drive down to the convenience store and fetch some. Only be ten minutes. Sit and sip your wine.' And he was gone.

The minute the note of his car engine died away she heard another car draw up outside and then the sound of the doorbell. Hugh had told her to be cautious of unexpected visitors so she peered through the peep-hole to check. She saw a white-haired man holding a bag. He didn't seem dangerous so she opened the door.

The man smiled and offered his hand. 'You'll be the nurse. Is Dr Ryder in too?'

'He's just slipped out for a moment.'

'My name is Michael Meadows—Micky to my friends. At the moment you're the biggest friends I've got. This afternoon you and Dr Ryder saved the life of Carl Meadows. He's my only son.'

'You'd better come in,' she said.

A quarter of an hour later she heard Luke's car arrive, then the rattle of his feet outside. 'Are you there, Kate?' she heard him call. He knew that she had a caller and she was pleased to hear the concern in his voice. Then he was in the kitchen, where she'd taken Micky.

'Luke, this is Micky Meadows, Carl's father. He's just come from the hospital. Carl is fine.'

The voice was steady, but she could feel the emotion throbbing underneath. 'Dr Ryder, I've come to thank you and this lady for keeping my son alive.'

Luke smiled. 'Mr Meadows, we were there. We were both happy to do what we could. I hope Carl makes a swift recovery.'

GILL SANDERSON　　157

'The doctors think he's well out of danger. Now they know he can suffer this reaction they're going to give him a whole pile of tests to find what he's allergic to, but he should be able to lead a normal life in future. Even carry on diving. He's just going to have to carry a pack of drugs for emergencies. Epinephrine and antihistamine, they said. And tourniquets as well.'

Both Luke and Kate knew what he was doing. His son's near-death had shocked him. Reciting medical precautions made the shock easier to take; the danger could be managed, in future something could be done.

'It was just a chance in a million,' Luke said soothingly. 'And now you've found there is a slight problem—well, you can deal with it.'

'We surely can. And we will.' He seemed a little calmer. 'Dr Ryder, I see you've just opened a bottle. I hope you won't think me rude but would you drink a glass of my wine? I've brought you a couple of bottles.'

Kate thought that she detected a slightly mischievous smile on Micky's face, but she couldn't tell why.

'We'll be happy to have a drink with you,' Luke said, obviously slightly surprised himself. 'Let me get three glasses.'

It turned out that it was a cool-bag that Micky had brought in. From it he took a bottle wrapped in a cloth and reached for the corkscrew that Luke handed him. Kate could tell by his dexterity that he was used to opening bottles. He half filled three glasses. 'I don't want to make a speech,' he said, 'but this wine comes with my thanks.'

Kate tasted hers. Luke had taught her how to taste wine, how to smell it first then let it linger in the mouth to catch all the flavours. Her first impression was of coolness. Then her mouth filled with an indescribable bouquet. She knew just enough to realise that she'd never drunk wine like this before.

She glanced across at Luke and nearly giggled. For once, the man with the stone face looked awestruck.

158 DR RYDER AND SON

Then the happiest of smiles spread across his face as he raised his glass again. 'I think this might be the finest Cabernet Sauvignon I've ever tasted,' he said. 'May I see the bottle?'

With a proud smile Micky pulled off the cloth and Luke took the bottle almost reverently. 'Hemp and Meadows Vineyard,' he read, then looked up, startled. 'It's not your vineyard?'

'It most certainly is. All mine. The Hemps died out years ago.'

'You're a lucky man.' Luke sipped again. 'I think I've tried most of the great French Cabernets, but I must say this beats them all.'

Micky looked gratified. 'That's a real compliment. I must be frank, Dr Ryder; I've got friends in the hospital Carl's been taken to, and one of them phoned to make a couple of enquiries about you. Apparently you're a connoisseur. I value your good opinion.'

'Well, thank you. What d'you think, Kate?'

'There's only one thing I can say. I like it.' Both men laughed.

'I wanted to call on you to give you my thanks,' Micky said, 'but now I want to go back to hospital to see Carl. My friend at hospital said I was on no account to offer you money for what you did—you were the kind of man to be insulted by the offer. I guess I could have worked that out for myself. But I have to give something. If you like, it's not for you, it's an offering to the gods for sparing my son.'

He took a case from his inside pocket and handed it to Kate. 'Native American art, Miss Storm. Navaho jewellery. May I say I think it will look well on you?'

She opened the leather case. Inside was a necklace— thirty or forty incredibly fine silver threads, all subtly different lengths, with occasional beads of turquoise. She couldn't resist taking it out, holding it to her neck and turning to the mirror on the wall.

GILL SANDERSON 159

'It's exquisite. But I didn't expect—' she started to protest, when Luke interrupted her.

'Imagine how you'd feel if it was your son.'

'Thank you very much,' she said quietly.

'And for you, Dr Ryder, there'll be a case of this wine shipped across to your home in England. It's usually reserved for family and very old clients. I know you'll appreciate it.'

For once Luke was nearly speechless. 'Thank you,' he managed to gasp.

'One more thing. You have a son, aged nine. I've got some Cabernet that's been down a couple of years; I'm keeping a case for him. It will be delivered on his eighteenth birthday. He can sell it then if he wants; it'll be worth a fortune. But if he's his father's son then I guess he'll drink it.'

Kate glanced at Luke. Outwardly he was unchanged, the same half-smile still on his lips. But she could feel the coldness emanating from him. His voice, however, remained calm and polite.

'Did you know that my son was very seriously ill?'

'Yes, I knew. Three hours ago my son was half a minute from death. There's always hope, Dr Ryder.'

Micky rose. Luke and Kate took him to the door, promising to keep in touch. Then they returned to the kitchen. She felt that they were in the calm before a storm.

'This wine is truly wonderful. I've had presents from patients before, but never anything like this.' With great precision he lifted his glass and sipped.

The words were pleasant, but by now she knew him well enough to feel the anger welling beneath. She decided that if they were going to have an argument they'd have it at once. 'I think his idea of putting wine down for Sean's eighteenth birthday is wonderful.'

'Yes. Did you tell him about Sean?' The words were Arctic in their coldness.

'I did tell him. He knew that Sean was ill, but I said

160 DR RYDER AND SON

that I still thought that putting wine down was a gift you would appreciate.'

'Appreciate!' The word was snarled out, and she shook inwardly. But the apparently cool comment that followed was worse. 'I suppose we could always drink it at his funeral.'

The words lashed at her, causing her almost physical pain. His father, calmly considering Sean's funeral— Sean, whom she loved. . . Then after the anguish came anger.

'Before you have a funeral you have to have a body,' she spat. 'And Sean's not dead! Do you understand that? He's not dead! He's alive, he's fighting, he's got a good chance. Your trouble is that you're too wrapped up in your own hurt feelings. One wife gone, one child seriously ill. Luke Ryder can't cope so he stops feeling altogether. If you expect the worst you won't be surprised. Haven't you ever heard of hope?'

She could feel the tears pouring down her face but she didn't care. She slumped in the chair opposite him, sobbing.

It seemed like ages that they sat there at each side of the kitchen table. He remained motionless, not even lifting the glass he held in one hand. When she glanced at him furtively she knew how his face would look: implacable, emotionless, showing as much feeling as a god carved in stone.

Eventually she took out her handkerchief and wiped her face. Her anger was diminishing. It struck her that, after all, she was a nurse, working for this man. Her outburst had been most unprofessional. Then she decided that she had meant every word.

'I'm sorry,' she said. 'What I said was uncalled for and most improper. I'll make sure it never happens again.'

She thought that he wasn't going to reply. The silence lengthened and she thought that the only thing to do would be to go to bed. Then he spoke.

'What you said might have been improper. I don't

GILL SANDERSON 161

know whether it was called for. The question is, was what you said true? Have I stopped feeling altogether?'

His voice was odd. She had expected it to be cold or angry, instead it was thoughtful. He sounded as if he genuinely wanted answers to his question.

When she made no answer he stood and walked round the table to her. She was crouched on her chair, head and shoulders bowed. To her great surprise he knelt on the floor in front of her, placing his hands on the front of her thighs. Gently he shook her.

'I don't know. I don't know anything. I'm just a nurse, that's all. It's wrong of me to get involved in patients' families.'

With one finger he lifted her chin. Then he stopped and kissed her on each cheek. 'You've been crying for me. Now, you're wrong on two counts. There's no such thing as *just* a nurse. And you are involved with me.'

'I only want you to hope. It's not a lot.'

'You're right. Now come on. I won't say cheer up; you might hit me. But bring your glass and come outside.'

She felt incapable of argument. Unresistingly she let him take her hand and lead her out onto the patio. Dusk was falling, the air was warm and full of the scent of pine trees from the neighbouring woods. They passed the heat of the barbecue; some distant part of her mind noted that it was now ready to cook. Was it so short a time since she'd lit it, since the two of them had been together and quietly happy?

He led her to a bench and sat her beside him, putting an arm round her and making her rest her head on his shoulder. 'We'll sit here a while and say nothing. We've had a hard day. I don't think you realise how tired we both are.'

'Doctors!' she snorted. 'They have to find a physical explanation for everything.'

He chuckled. 'Just sit still.'

It was comforting half sitting, half lying there. Her head rested against the great muscles of his chest and

162 DR RYDER AND SON

shoulder; dimly she was aware of the beating of his heart. She thought of nothing. And in time her own heartbeat slowed and the storm in her emotions calmed. He didn't say anything but the silence between them wasn't hostile. Occasionally he lifted his glass to his lips, while with the other hand he caressed her back.

'I'm hungry,' she said abruptly, lifting her head.

'I'm hungry too,' he agreed.

'Well, I've made a salad and the bread's ready for cutting. What about this new wonder taste you're going to offer me? Abalone?'

He responded to her change of mood, the smile in his eyes telling her that he recognised it. 'It's all ready to cook. D'you want to lay the table?' They were moving together again, previous arguments forgotten.

He looked at the barbecue and frowned. 'I can still grill the abalone. We'll not eat it all, but it's just as good cold.'

'Whatever you like. Just so long as we eat soon.' She busied herself setting the metal table out on the patio while he laid the shellfish on the grill.

It was magical eating outside. In the distance was the glow of San Francisco, while above them was the blue velvet of the night sky, pierced by the silver of stars. Luke had recorked Micky's bottle; it wasn't suitable for fish. Instead he opened a bottle of sparkling wine from a neighbouring vineyard.

'Now, what do you think of abalone?'

Cautiously she tasted a mouthful. It wasn't tremendously fishy—which pleased her. The texture was strange. And the taste was subtle. Thinking that she quite liked it, she tried another mouthful. Now this time she definitely liked it. She'd try a bit more.

After a while she looked up to see him smiling at her. 'You like it,' he said.

'It's the oddest thing I've ever eaten. But oh, yes, I do like it.'

It was a simple meal, but one that she knew she'd never forget.

After they had finished she made the Colombian coffee that he liked and carried the cafetière onto the patio. He was lying on one of the loungers and he pulled another to his side so that she could lie next to him.

She poured him a cup and he reclined with it resting on his stomach. 'Lie down and look at the sky, Kate,' he said. 'It's calming. Just think of the distance between us and the nearest star. Doesn't it make you feel insignificant?'

'Certainly not. Do you think there's a little green man on the nearest star, looking at us and feeling insignificant? If he's not going to feel insignificant, then neither am I.'

'Hmm! Some Greek philosophers thought women didn't have souls. There are times when I could agree.'

'I'll bet they were male Greek philosophers. It *is* very nice lying out here.'

They sipped their coffee. 'What are you thinking?' she asked after a pause.

'I was remembering the last time we lay out in the open air. Up over the wolds. I persuaded you to take off your shirt. You looked gorgeous.'

She decided not to comment so he asked, 'What are *you* thinking of?'

'I'm thinking of Clare Hall and her philosophy. Seize the day. Take what you can while you can; there might not be another chance.'

'It could be a recipe for disaster,' he warned.

'It could. But I think the opposite is far more soul-destroying.'

'Seize the day,' he murmured. He drank the last of his coffee.

They were lying side by side on their loungers. When he reached over to take her hand she let him, unresisting. I talked him into this, she thought. Or did I talk myself into it?

At first he did nothing but kiss her hand, turning it so that his lips brushed the palm, the soft skin inside her wrist, the tip of each finger. It was gentle but exciting, like the promise of more. She stared straight upwards, seeking familiar constellations in the sky. Then her eyes closed and all her mind was on the man next to her.

There was a creak from the lounger next to her as he rolled on his side, still clutching her hand. But he was closer now, and he feathered kisses up the inside of her arm, so slowly that it was the sweetest of tortures. Her dress was sleeveless, so in time he reached her shoulder, his tongue flicking at the tiny crease between her arm and the top of her body.

It was time for her to act. She would not lie here, merely compliant. If there were decisions to be made, she would make them too. She turned her head, so that she was facing his.

His face was in shadow. But she could see the curve of his lips, and the dim pinpricks of stars reflected in his eyes. She reached up to rub her hand through his hair, then let her fingers stray over the hard planes of his face.

His kiss was at first gentle. They lay there side by side, their lips touching, but no other part of their bodies. Then he leaned over and pulled her to him; his kiss grew more urgent. In her turn she wrapped her arms round him.

For a while they strained together, his tongue probing into the sensitive skin of her mouth, the muscles of his chest crushing her breasts. Then, firmly, he pushed her from him and slumped back on his lounger, only his hoarse breath an indication of what he was feeling.

'This isn't fair to you,' he said huskily. 'We should stop now.'

'I think it wouldn't be fair if we *did* stop now,' she protested. 'Luke, I'm adult. I know what I'm doing. Don't you want me?'

GILL SANDERSON

165

His voice was a low cry. 'Of course I want you. But. . .'

She leaned over him and kissed him. 'Then we'll go inside.'

'Do you mean that?'

'I said we'll go inside. To your bedroom. Or to mine if you want.'

He still made no move so she went on, 'I know what you're going to say: you can't offer me anything. Well, I know that, and I don't expect anything. Tomorrow you're back at work and I'm Sean's nurse again. But we have now. So let's seize the day—or, to be more accurate, let's seize the night. No expectations, no recriminations.'

He stood and held down his hand to her. 'Come with me, then,' he said softly.

He led her into the house, up the stairs to the redwood door to her bedroom. There, awkwardly, she stopped. 'Luke, what I said wasn't all bravado. But I don't want to get pregnant.'

He smiled at her wryly. 'We'll take precautions; I've got something. When we came here I thought that perhaps. . . Well, a man can dream.' He pushed the door open.

This room was bigger than hers. She could dimly make out French windows opening onto a balcony, trees outlined against the glow of the city in the distance. He flicked a switch and the room was a pattern of shadows and bars of light.

She was nervous now. He seemed to sense it and pulled her to him, letting her head rest on his shoulder. For what seemed like ages they stood there without moving. After a while she lifted her mouth to be kissed. He kissed her, gently at first, and more long moments passed.

Slowly their kisses became more passionate. His arms round her tightened, pulling her to him, and she could feel the undeniable proof of his feelings. In her turn she

166   DR RYDER AND SON

felt her engorged nipples rubbing against her dress.

It seemed as if they had all the time in the world. He stepped back from her and with fumbling fingers undid one by one the buttons down the front of her dress. Then he slipped it from her and leaned over to kiss her shoulders. Her underskirt dropped in a lacy puddle round her feet and she kicked off her shoes.

She wondered if unconsciously she had been expecting this earlier. She'd put on her filmiest underwear—matching bra and briefs in ivory silk.

'You're still dressed,' she murmured to him, and pulled his white polo shirt over his head. Once again she admired his body—the lithe muscles, the waist, the fine hair fanning from the thin line disappearing into his trousers. In her turn she kissed his chest, her lips caressed by the soft down. She heard his quick indrawn breath as her tongue lingered over his nipples. 'Are you as sensitive as me there?' she asked.

Urgently he dragged her back to him, his kiss giving her a hint of the way he was holding himself back. His hands pulled at the catch of her bra. Then he stood back to let it fall down her arms. 'How beautiful you are,' he muttered.

He eased her backwards onto the bed. Then he leaned over her and kissed her breasts, taking them in his mouth as his tide of passion mounted. She felt a thrill of excitement as his teeth bit, but oh, so gently.

As he lifted his head to kiss her lips again his body eased up and onto hers. She heard his rasping breath. Then he slid his hands down to her hips and took off her briefs. She moved languorously to help him, and then she was lying there naked.

For a while he was just a silhouette against the starlight from the window. There was a rustling of clothing, and he was naked too. Even in the semi-darkness she could see his maleness. Then he was on the bed by her, and she found that she was panting gently.

He lay by her side, kissing her. His hands roamed her

GILL SANDERSON

body; she hadn't guessed what pleasure his soft touch could give her. The inside of her arms, the cleft between her breasts, the line of her waist—all were explored and all gave delight.

He laid his hand on her leg and as his fingers stroked the soft flesh on the inside of her thigh she flinched at first. Her heart beat more rapidly. His hand reached higher and she felt half fear, half exquisite pleasure. Then slowly the fear left her, and only the pleasure remained. She knew that he was trying to please her, and in her turn she reached down to grasp him.

'Luke, my darling Luke,' she moaned. 'Now, darling, now!'

His body was suddenly poised above hers and for a moment she felt the tiniest apprehension. It passed as he bent his head to kiss her. She reached up to clutch him and pull him to her. She sighed in ecstasy.

At first there was the most negligible of pains—and then they were together.

She revelled in their possession of each other, knowing instinctively what to do, how to move in time with him, till the pleasure was almost more than she could bear. It felt so good, so natural.

It seemed no time at all before his desire was rushing to a climax. She moaned with pleasure at the crescendo, and then he gave a great cry as his passion, held in check for so long, flooded into her.

He fell, his head on her shoulder, and gently she stroked the sweat-dewed muscles of his back.

'You, Kate, are wonderful,' he said after a while. 'I've never. . .never felt anything like that.'

'Nor me,' she said drily. 'It was a completely new experience.'

The meaning of her words slowly became clear to him. 'New experience? You mean you were a. . .?'

'Yes, I was a virgin.'

'I didn't know! I—'

She kissed him. 'It doesn't matter,' she interrupted.

168 DR RYDER AND SON

'It was wonderful, and so are you. Now be quiet a while. I don't want to talk just now.'

'Hmm,' he grumbled, but his head fell back on her shoulder and there was peace between them.

She lay there happily with his arm crooked over her shoulders and her leg bent over his. From the open windows the smallest of breezes cooled their bodies. She found this calmness nearly as marvellous as the passion that had preceded it. Occasionally he lifted his head to kiss her.

She wasn't sure how long they lay there. He rolled onto his side and stretched his arm to stroke her side slowly—a soothing, rhythmic movement. After a while the stroking became more than pleasant—it became exciting. 'Luke, what are you doing?' she questioned, but she had already guessed.

'Nice, isn't it?' he said.

His hand trailed down to caress her breasts and she shuddered. Her breathing grew more rapid; she felt the pulse beat in her wrist, her neck. The feeling of luxurious calm was passing; in its place was mounting excitement again. He kissed her, his tongue penetrating her readily open mouth. 'Luke,' she called.

Once again he was poised above her. And she smiled as he leaned towards her.

It was different this time. Something told her that he was more restrained. Welling within her were feelings that she'd only dreamed of, an excitement beyond anything known before. And eventually it was she who screamed his name in a delirium of joy, half-aware that he was sharing her climax.

Then they lay side by side. 'Sleep now,' he said, and she slept.

Unusually, in the morning she woke before he did. She tiptoed to fetch her robe, then made two cups of coffee and took them back to his bedroom.

GILL SANDERSON 169

'Morning, sleepyhead,' she said, and easily avoided the grab he made for her.

'I get up first,' he pointed out.

'Not this morning. This morning is different, like last night was different. Now you drink your coffee while I have a shower.'

Ten minutes later she returned to find him still in bed, a speculative look on his face. She'd pulled on a tracksuit. He was sitting up, unshaven, his hair tousled. But the sight of his muscular shoulders and broad chest made her remember the night before, and her determination wavered.

'Move over, but don't get any ideas,' she said, and slipped into bed by his side.

'Don't get any ideas?' he scoffed, and kissed her.

'Now that's it,' she said, after two minutes' heaven. 'We're going to be serious.'

'I was never more serious in my life.'

'Shut up and listen.' She had to get the tone just right. She had to be firm and yet she didn't want him thinking that in any way she regretted what they'd done.

'I said yesterday that there'd be no recriminations and no regrets, and I meant it. Though who knows what we might think in England? But for the rest of our stay here Sean's going to be with us. We will behave just as we did before. I don't want you to talk about last night; if you can I want you to forget it.'

He shook his head. 'I'll never forget it, Kate; you know that. But I'll stick to your ground rules. I won't mention it. Now. . .'

'Now is the morning after last night,' she said, 'and you told me you had an appointment. You're going to be late.' She climbed out of bed. 'I'll make you another coffee.'

'Kate?' At the sound of his voice she turned; there was an infinity of meaning in his calling her name. But perhaps he saw the pain that she was trying so hard to

170 DR RYDER AND SON

conceal. His eyes searched her face then he merely said, 'I'd appreciate another coffee.'

A quarter of an hour later he left. She carefully kept at the far side of the kitchen from him; she thought that she wouldn't be able to bear it if he kissed her goodbye. But he didn't try.

When he was gone she went back to his bedroom, stripped off her tracksuit and crept into the bed. She put her face to the impression his head had made, and very faintly she could detect the exciting smell of his body. Then, bitterly, she wept.

CHAPTER TEN

KATE still loved flying, especially club class, but travelling back wasn't as enjoyable as travelling out. Sean was just as excited and Luke was pleasant and polite, but she had a feeling of things ending. She'd always known that her time in America was something extra and that she was not to expect that time to continue. And now it was drawing to a close.

Would Luke say anything to her?

Those twenty-four hours spent with Luke had been the most memorable of her life. The diving, saving Carl's life, the wine, the barbecue and then the ecstasy of the night—she relived them each day.

There was a bargain between her and Luke not to mention what had happened. He had been busy at work, of course, and she had had her hands full with Sean. But she would have liked just the tiniest indication from him that what had happened meant the same to him as it did to her. Possibly it didn't. She stared gloomily out of the plane window as the thought struck her.

Harry Wentworth met them at Manchester and they were whisked smartly back to Yannthorpe. Lucy was now convalescing with her sister in Wales, but Harry had arranged for the house to be warmed and food brought in. The weather was good, the house as lovely as ever; Sean, Luke and Harry seemed pleased to be with her. But she knew that there was something wrong. She was relieved when Luke suggested that they were all jet lagged and should go to bed early.

In the morning there was a message from Marion. She wanted Luke to bring Sean in for a check-up. It wasn't necessary but she'd like just to be certain. After breakfast

172 DR RYDER AND SON

Luke and Sean set off for the hospital and Kate mooned about the house, dissatisfied with herself and the world in general.

The phone rang in the middle of the afternoon. And when she heard Luke's voice her heart bumped, just as it always did.

'Kate?' Just the one syllable in his dark voice and she felt better.

'That's me. Present in body if not entirely in spirit. I think that's halfway across the Atlantic.'

He laughed. 'So you're feeling disorientated too? I know exactly what you mean. Never mind; it'll soon pass. A couple of days and— Oh, hang on a minute . . .'

She knew that he was phoning from a ward somewhere; she could hear the hum of activity behind him. He'd turned away from the phone and she heard him say, 'I want these tests repeated, please. I know it's troublesome, but we have to be absolutely certain. . .'

Then he was back on the line to her. 'Sorry about that. The work's been piling up. Why I phoned—Sean's not coming home tonight. Marion wants to keep him and I might as well stay here too. I'm mad busy. I'll come home tomorrow about midday. You'll be all right on your own?'

'I'll be all right,' she acknowledged, but feeling that she'd have rather he had made an effort and come to see her.

'Settled, then. See you.'

He rang off, leaving her feeling more dissatisfied than ever.

As promised, he returned next day at midday. Tentatively she'd made him a light lunch—just ham with a salad—but he said he wasn't hungry; he would shower and change then go straight back to work.

'Actually, I wanted to talk to you,' he said, and the sombre way he spoke gripped her heart with a hand of ice.

'Is Sean all right?' she demanded. 'Has anything turned up on the tests?'

He hesitated. 'Sean is fine. In fact Marion was so impressed with his account of holidaying in Yosemite that she's arranging a similar trip. He's going sailing round Scotland next week.'

His face reminded her of when she'd first met him— an expresssionless stone mask. He went on, 'Now I'll go and have a shower and change, then there's something I must say to you.'

She could neither think nor act. When he returned ten minutes later she hadn't moved from her chair.

He sat opposite her. Without comment she noted the dampness of his hair, the faint tang of the expensive cologne he used after shaving, the pristine whiteness of his fresh shirt. These were things that she'd got used to over the past two weeks. They'd become part of her life.

'Kate, it's over. It would be cruel and dishonest of me to pretend that our relationship has been just one between. . .well, a nurse and a family. It's been much, much more. But I've tried to make it clear that there's no way I could enter into any. . .commitment.'

'You want me to go.' It was a simple, flat statement. For too long she'd been refusing to face up to this happening; now she had to.

'I don't *want* you to go. Obviously you can stay here as long as you like. But you won't be needed to look after Sean. Your nursing work is finished.'

'So there's nothing to keep me here.'

For a second she thought that she saw a flicker of discomfort in that obdurate face, but it was quickly gone. 'Not really, no.'

The silence between them stretched on. He reached into his inside pocket, took out a cheque-book and started to write. 'I'm going to pay you to the end of this month and for another six weeks. If there's any problem getting your old job back then please get in touch; I'm sure I'll be able to sort things out.'

174 DR RYDER AND SON

'It's always an embarrassment when you have to dismiss staff, isn't it?' she said bitingly. She was hoping to find anger inside her—anything but this feeling of chill desolation.

'You are not staff and I'm not dismissing you.'

She picked up the cheque. 'This looks pretty final to me. Generous, but final.'

'I'm sorry, Kate. I know what you must be feeling, but—'

'You don't! You can have no idea what I'm feeling!' It burst out before she could stop herself. Then, as the anger bit into her, she went on, 'Thank you for the money. Tell me, if I need a reference in future, can I give your name? After all, I've provided all sorts of *services* for you and your family.'

She hadn't thought it possible that a man could radiate such fury without a muscle of his face moving. His voice was calm, though there was the rasp of temper in it. 'That is unworthy of you, Kate, and you know it.'

It was no good—she couldn't get angry. 'Yes, it was,' she agreed. 'You never talked me into anything; you even warned me against talking myself into things.'

Somehow she stood; somehow she even managed a tight smile. 'Say goodbye to Sean for me,' she said. 'In hospital I always found it better not to try to keep in touch with patients when they left; it was a professional relationship, after all. So I won't phone you. Now, if you'd like to get to work, I'll go and pack. I'll be gone by late this afternoon.'

'Kate, there's no need to—'

'There's every need! I've never asked you for anything, but I'm asking now! Just go and I'll get out of your life for good. I can see no reason why we should ever meet again.'

There was a last moment of stillness. She knew that he was looking at her; she kept her eyes fixed downwards. Then there was the sound of footsteps

GILL SANDERSON 175

disappearing, the slam of the front door, the gentle roar of a car engine.

Inaction would only make the agony harder to bear. Kate went upstairs to pack.

Some children adapted quickly to life in the ward, some did not. Nine-year-old Alice Dixon had been terrified when she'd come into hospital and she'd never got used to it. Of all the nurses and staff on the ward, only Kate managed to get through to Alice, only Kate could win a tremulous smile. It was obvious, therefore, that Kate should accompany Alice on her first, frightening visit to the radiotherapist.

'The lady's just going to take a picture of the inside of you,' Kate said encouragingly, 'and you're going to have to squish yourself up very small.'

She helped Alice undress and sit on a small chair. Then she and Maddy Clein, the radiotherapist, carefully positioned little test discs on each side of Alice's head, body and legs. Bags filled with silicon were placed round other parts of Alice; they absorbed radiation at the same rate as human tissue. Finally Alice was made to clutch her legs to her chest and bend over. Maddy made the last few precise adjustments to Alice's position while Kate kept up a flow of encouragement.

'You're a very brave girl, Alice, and just for a minute you're going to keep still as a mouse. I'm going to be a big cat and I'm going to hide behind that wall over there and look for you. Miaow! I want a little mouse! Now you be still, Alice.'

Alice giggled but she did as Kate said, and a few minutes later Maddy nodded approvingly. 'That should do, Kate. You're a wonder with these children.'

'All part of the job.' Kate yawned. 'When will you have the results?'

'In a few days. Then we'll calculate the proper dosage.' This had been a test; the little discs on one side of Alice's body had measured how much radiation

176   DR RYDER AND SON

entered her, the corresponding discs on the other side of the body had measured how much radiation had been absorbed. Since there was only one radiation source, the silicon bags were to make sure that all Alice's body presented a uniform thickness. It was a much used technique—but with a frightened patient it could be a difficult one.

'So we'll see you in a day or two. That wasn't too bad, was it, Alice? We'll come back to see Maddy again in a day or two.'

Her little patient was dressed and helped back onto her trolley. Then there was the trek back to the ward.

She'd been back on Aladdin Ward for three months now. She had her old room, the same circle of friends, the same exhausting work round. In some ways it was good to be back; she knew what she was doing, was confident of her own worth. She must have relaxed in the few weeks she'd been away; certainly there was no sign of burn-out now. She went about her tasks with an almost feverish intensity.

And yet, underneath, she knew all was not well. She missed Sean, Lucy, the life at Yannthorpe. She missed Luke—but she wouldn't let herself think about him. What was done was done. In time the pain would go away. But it didn't; even after three months her memories were bright, as if etched by acid into her brain.

She'd heard nothing of Luke, and had deliberately made no enquiries. She couldn't even bring up the subject with Mike Hamilton; he was on a year's sabbatical exchange at a hospital in Australia. So she worked on, doing overtime, filling in, asking for unpopular shift times—anything that would stop her thinking or remembering.

When it happened it came as a shock. She was to accompany Judith Doyle, the senior registrar, on a ward round. Judith tapped on the door, then swept into her little room. 'Ready when you are,' she said to Kate. 'We have a

GILL SANDERSON 177

visitor for the day. This is Marion Pitts, from the Wolds and Dales over the Pennines. Have you got the case notes?'

Medicine was a small world; it had had to happen some time. She'd had to run into someone who knew Luke. But she'd always got on with Marion; they'd been friends.

'We've already met,' she explained to Judith. 'Hello, Marion.'

'Sister Storm,' was the cold acknowledgement. Kate's outstretched hand was apparently not noticed as the two doctors bent over the case notes.

She'd been snubbed; she wondered why. But Judith wanted to get on with her round, so there was no time to think.

However, as the round progressed, as they moved from bed to bed, Kate found herself getting angry. Judith was the doctor who diagnosed and prescribed, but she, Kate, was the nurse responsible for the care and well-being of their charges. There was a dual responsibility. Kate knew that she did a good job and it rankled that Marion should treat her as a lesser being.

When they'd finished the round Kate invited the two doctors to coffee. No sooner had she poured three cups than a patient's father arrived and Judith excused herself for five minutes. This was Kate's chance; she was alone with Marion.

'How is Sean?' she asked politely.

The question seemed to annoy Marion. 'As well as can be expected,' she snapped. 'He did ask for you quite a lot. It wouldn't have hurt you to say goodbye to him if you *had* to go.'

Kate wanted to say that it would have hurt her an awful lot, but she didn't. 'Did he enjoy his sailing trip to Scotland?' she persisted.

'What sailing trip to Scotland? He's not been out of hospital since you left him.'

'But Luke said. . .I wasn't needed. . .you'd arranged

178   DR RYDER AND SON

that. . .' There was something wrong. Marion had put down her cup and was looking at her curiously.

'Please, how *is* Sean?' Kate asked. 'I really want to know.'

Marion now seemed more sad than angry. 'He's relapsed again. There's always hope, I suppose—but very little now.'

Grief and anger welled up in Kate—an unholy mix of emotions so powerful that she could hardly speak. 'I didn't know,' she gasped eventually. 'When we came back from America, Luke said—he said that Sean was all right now and I wouldn't be needed any more.'

'He said what? I'd just taken a bone-marrow sample. I told him Sean was in real danger.'

The two women stared at each other, each busy with her own thoughts. Marion spoke first. 'Luke told me that you'd had an offer of a job that was just too good to refuse. But you had to go at once. I must say, I was surprised that you left just when you could have been most use.'

Dully Kate said, 'He told me that Sean's progress was fine, that since there was no work for me I might as well go.'

'But why? I just don't believe you'd fallen down in your nursing duties—anyway, Luke would have told me. It must have been. . . Oh, I see. It was you and Luke, wasn't it? You'd fallen in love.'

'I fell in love,' Kate said bitterly, 'but Luke didn't. He could have kept me on; I wouldn't have been an embarrassment to him.'

For a moment Marion played with her cup, turning it round and round with one finger. Then she said, 'It's not my business, and all my training tells me not to get involved, but I think you're wrong. Over the last three months he's been absolute hell to work with. And it's not only worry over Sean; he can deal with that. It looks as if he's missing you.'

'Then why did he send me away?'

GILL SANDERSON 179

'Only you can tell. You do know, don't you?'

'I think I do now,' Kate said slowly. Out of the chaos of her conflicting emotions understanding was slowly growing. 'He knew I was getting fond of Sean. And he didn't want to put me through the suffering of watching him get more and more ill. The arrogant swine!'

'Luke has never hesitated to do what he thinks is right, no matter what anyone else thinks,' Marion observed drily. 'When he makes up his mind, it stays made.'

'Just so long as he doesn't try to make up *my* mind.'

Marion stood. 'I must go, Kate. Two things first. I'm sorry I was so rude to you; by now I should know never to make judgements without knowing all the facts. Secondly, don't be too hard on Luke. If you have suffered, I bet he's suffered twice as much. You are going to see him, aren't you?'

'You bet I am.' Emotion was getting too much for Kate; she stepped forward and hugged Marion. 'Thanks for helping me, Marion. Just one thing—don't tell Luke you've seen me.'

'He's been in London for two days, doesn't even know I've come here. And, whatever happens, good luck.' And Marion was gone.

Kate sat and tried to make sense of her whirling emotions. By turns she was angry, hopeful, depressed. One thing was certain: Luke Ryder and she had to meet. If nothing else, there were a few home truths she had to tell him.

It had been easy to get time off; she was owed a lot of favours. Two days after seeing Marion, at the end of a morning shift, she was setting off over the Pennines again. Marion had been a useful ally. On the telephone she had told Kate that Luke would certainly be at home, alone, at Yannthorpe that evening. Lucy had gone to visit her sister again. Yes, it would be fine for Kate to come into hospital to visit Sean first.

There wasn't much traffic; she was soon out of the

180 DR RYDER AND SON

smoky town and climbing into the clear air of the Pennines. It struck her that each time she'd taken this route her life had changed. Was it going to change again?

Marion had warned her about the change in Sean, and her professional experience told her what to expect. But even so his appearance wrenched at her heart. He was heavily drugged but she thought that he recognised her and he seemed pleased to see her. She promised to come to see him again.

It was now late summer and she thought that she'd never seen the country look so beautiful. She drove through well-remembered villages, and then there was Yannthorpe, and outside was Luke's car. She coasted to a silent halt and prepared to do battle.

The front door was open so she stepped inside. It gave her an odd pang to see the once familiar panelling, to smell again the scent of pot-pourri and polish. 'Anyone home?' she called; there was no answer.

She peered in the living room, the kitchen. Then, inevitably, she moved to the conservatory where so many of her happy hours had been spent.

Luke was there, asleep. He was slumped in one of the cane chairs, his feet propped on a coffee-table. To one side was a glass of milk and a half-eaten sandwich— just a slab of ham thrust between two slices of bread.

He must have carried on working as soon as he'd arrived home. There were papers scattered around him and he was still wearing his formal dark suit. Usually he changed into something casual when he came in.

For minutes she stood there looking at him. Asleep, he looked defenceless. She could see the sensuous curve of his lips; they weren't now tightened into his forbidding, stony expression. Perhaps there were additional lines at the corners of his eyes and round his mouth; he looked weary. For a moment, of all the conflicting emotions she felt pity was strongest, and she wanted to hold him to her, to comfort him.

His eyes flicked open, tried to focus on her. She could

see bewilderment chasing across his face; he didn't know why she was there. 'Kate?' he mumbled, and she thought that she could hear his pleasure at her being there. It soon passed. His head lifted and he stared at her.

'What the hell are you doing here?' he asked angrily.

'That's the Luke we all love. No hello, no how have you been, no would you like a drink. Just what the hell are you doing here.'

'I'm sorry,' he said, not seeming very sorry at all. 'I just didn't expect to see you.'

'Ever again?'

'Precisely. I thought I made it clear that our relationship was finished.'

'You made it abundantly clear. Now tell me how Sean is. And this time don't lie to me!'

He pushed himself up in his chair, his feet thudding to the floor. 'You know about Sean, then?'

'I visited him in hospital this afternoon. I like to think he just recognised me and was pleased to see me.'

'He's been sedated, but it's possible. Now, I'm sorry I'm being such a poor host. Would you like a cup of tea or something?'

'Don't talk to me about tea!' she shouted. 'We are talking about your son. I want to know how he is.'

When he replied his tone was impersonal, as if he was distancing himself from what he was saying. 'Sean's prognosis isn't good. Chemotherapy and radiation have largely failed. His only chance would be a bone-marrow transplant, but we can't find a suitable donor. I've searched every database in the world.'

'I see,' she said. It was just what Marion had told her. 'Now tell me why you lied to me. Why did you say Sean was better when he was in fact worse?'

He shrugged. 'I wanted to save you pain. The result was the same: since he was in hospital there was no work for you.'

'So I was nothing to you but a paid employee?'

'Well. . .'

182   DR RYDER AND SON

'Getting the truth out of you is worse than pulling teeth. I'll tell you why you got rid of me. You didn't want another Maria, another woman who couldn't take the suffering of watching her child die.'

Now he too was angry. He leaped to his feet and strode over to her. Gripping her by the arms, he said, 'So you think you're entitled to absolute honesty?'

'It's about time,' she said.

'Then I'll be honest. You're the one woman I've ever met who I'd want to spend the rest of my life with. But my life is Sean's. He's not your son and I couldn't and I won't ask you to go through what I'm going through.'

Her heart pounded as she stared at the anguished face in front of her. 'You won't ask me to suffer what you're suffering?' she demanded. 'How do you think I've felt in the last three months?'

'If you've felt anything like me,' he said quietly, 'then I'm sorry. Please, Kate, accept that I was doing what I thought was best for you. And it hurt.'

'In future, when you think you're doing what is best for me you can ask me first. Right.' She stepped closer to him, wrapped her arms round him. Gazing into his eyes, she said, 'Luke Ryder, I've loved you since I first saw you in that hospital ward. I think you love me. So marry me!' She leaned forward and kissed his bewildered face.

For a moment she felt a curious sense of detachment. There were two bodies locked together. Hers was soft and stretching towards him, his was hard. It wasn't like her, but she had gambled her pride, her dignity, perhaps even her chance of any future happiness on this one mad throw of the dice. How would he respond?

Time seemed frozen. He wouldn't need to speak his reply; she'd know it from the tensed, hard-muscled frame that she was clutching with such intensity.

He sighed; she felt his chest rising, and then as he breathed out his body relaxed. One of his arms clipped round her waist, the other moved up to caress the back of her neck. He pulled her to him. It's going to be all right, she thought wildly to herself.

They stood there without moving. He kissed her, gently, undemandingly. She felt as if she'd returned home after desolate months abroad. Then he broke off the kiss and led her to sit by him on the wickerwork couch.

'I want you to do something for me,' he said. 'I want you to withdraw the offer you just made.'

She looked at him, not really alarmed. 'I meant it, you know.'

'I know you did. But I'm a traditionalist at heart, and I believe there are things that only men can—or should—do.'

'You're just a male chauvinistic pig,' she said happily. 'All right, if it will make you happy, don't marry me. Offer withdrawn.'

'Wait here.' He rose and disappeared inside the house.

She didn't know where he was going, what he was going to do. It was as if she'd expended all her energy; now she would tranquilly await what would come next.

He returned to sit by her. 'My great-grandmother was a suffragette; she went to prison in 1912. I think she would have liked you. You obviously have certain qualities in common.' He took a battered leather box from his pocket and opened it. 'This was her ring. I want you to wear it until I can buy you a new one. I want you to marry me, Kate.'

It was an old ring, well worn. Little leaves and tendrils of gold twined round a central dark blue amethyst. She thought that she'd never seen anything so beautiful in her life.

For once she could think of nothing to say. Over the past few minutes there had been so much said that she needed relief. He sensed her fatigue and wrapped an arm round her. 'It's a big decision,' he said. 'Take your time.'

They sat close together, silently but happily. He took her left hand and stroked it. At first she kept it closed.

DR RYDER AND SON

Then her hand opened, her fingers straightened and spread and he slipped on the ring. It fitted perfectly. 'I'll marry you,' she said. He kissed her again.

It was blissful just being there, half sitting, half lying, knowing that he was hers. There was no further need for pain or strife or argument. 'I feel happy,' she said. 'Not ecstatically happy—that'll come tomorrow—but calmly happy. Everything's going to be all right now.'

He squeezed her. 'You've always known what I'm thinking. I feel the same way too.'

The evening was quiet. She cooked him supper while he sat in the corner of the kitchen. Their conversation was idle, each catching up on what the other had done over the last three months. They made no plans, spoke of nothing troublesome. She felt like the captain of a ship who had sailed into the calmness of a harbour after a long and stormy voyage. It was good to be home. The rejoicing could start tomorrow.

He took her to bed quite early. When he came back from his shower she was lying there naked, and she thrilled as she heard the hiss of his swiftly drawn-in breath. She held her left hand out to him so that her ring shone in the light of the bedside lamp and said mischievously, 'I feel quite proper now. I'm almost a married woman.'

'We'll just pretend you are.' He stooped to kiss her as she lay there, her hands now behind her head. Then his lips trailed down her body, kissing shoulders, pink-tipped breasts, the gentle curve of her stomach, and beyond.

This time their lovemaking was gentle. Or it started that way. For a while they were content just to be together, to explore each other's body, to give and to take pleasure. But then soon her body arched beneath his and she cried his name. Passion throbbed through her again and again in a climax lasting like the Pacific waves she'd seen pounding the rocky American coast.

'We'll do it again tomorrow,' she promised sleepily, and her eyes closed.

At four thirty in the morning the phone rang.

She was instantly awake. At this hour of the morning it had to be bad news. Beside her Luke turned to the phone. She stroked the long muscles of his back, then wrapped an arm round his waist. She was with him; whatever bad news there was they would share.

Somehow Luke kept his voice calm. 'Marion? You're up late—or early if you like.'

Marion? It had to be news about Sean. Had there been a relapse? She pulled herself closer to Luke, hoping that her presence would bring him comfort.

'Well, thank you for letting me know. . . Of course you did right waking me. I'll be in first thing in the morning. By the way, I'll have some news for you. Say hello to Kate.'

He rolled over, holding the phone. 'Say hello to Marion,' he invited Kate.

'Er—hello, Marion,' she said uncertainly.

She heard a chuckle. 'I hope no one's listening in on this line. Nice to hear from you, Kate. Perhaps see you soon.' The line went dead.

'Was it about Sean?' she asked, unable to make out why Luke seemed so unconcerned.

'It was about Sean. Marion had just been woken up, so she decided I should be woken up.'

'You don't seem upset about it.'

He grabbed her and hugged her, so hard that she felt the breath squeezed from her lungs. 'She'd just had a phone call from America. From Hugh Stenson. He was so excited that he didn't bother about the time difference. You know we were searching databases for a bone-marrow match for Sean? Well, Hugh has found one.'

'An exact match?' That would be almost impossible.

'No, but the computer says it's good enough. Hugh's

186 DR RYDER AND SON

having the marrow harvested and flown over. I can hardly believe it; I'd given up hope.'

'I told you, there's always hope,' she said. Deep inside her she felt a happiness bubbling that was almost uncontainable.

'Now we can plan the rest of our lives together.' Again he leaned over to kiss her.

'It's half past four in the morning,' she said some delirious moments later. 'What do you want to plan now?'

'We can plan something. We have a Sean already. What about a Marion or a James? And Joanne or Alex? Or. . .well, you think of names.'

'A boy should be called after his father,' she whispered. 'And a girl. . . Luke? Is this what you call planning?'

His lips had trailed a line of fire down across her neck. Her body arched to meet his.

'This isn't planning. It's action,' he said.

MILLS & BOON®

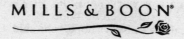

Books for enjoyment this month...

CRISIS FOR CASSANDRA	Abigail Gordon
PRESCRIPTION—ONE HUSBAND	Marion Lennox
WORTH WAITING FOR	Josie Metcalfe
DR RYDER AND SON	Gill Sanderson

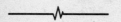

Treats in store!

Watch next month for these absorbing stories...

TRUSTING DR SCOTT	Mary Hawkins
PRESCRIPTION—ONE BRIDE	Marion Lennox
TAKING RISKS	Sharon Kendrick
PERFECT PRESCRIPTION	Carol Wood

Available from:
W.H. Smith, John Menzies, Volume One, Forbuoys, Martins,
Woolworths, Tesco, Asda, Safeway and other paperback stockists.

Readers in South Africa - write to:
IBS, Private Bag X3010, Randburg 2125.

MILLS & BOON®

Anne Mather

Collection

This summer Mills & Boon brings you a powerful
collection of three passionate love stories from
an outstanding author of romance:

**Tidewater Seduction
Rich as Sin
Snowfire**

576 pages of passion, drama and
compelling story lines.

Available: August 1996

*Available from WH Smith, John Menzies, Volume One, Forbuoys,
Martins, Woolworths, Tesco, Asda, Safeway and other
paperback stockists.*

MILLS & BOON

From Here To Paternity

Don't miss our great new series featuring fantastic men who eventually make fabulous fathers.

Some seek paternity, some have it thrust upon them—all will make it—whether they like it or not!

In September '96, look out for:

Finn's Twins!
by Anne McAllister

Available from WH Smith, John Menzies, Volume One, Forbuoys, Martins, Woolworths, Tesco, Asda, Safeway and other paperback stockists.

MILLS & BOON®

Back by Popular Demand

BETTY NEELS

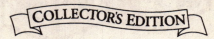

A collector's edition of favourite titles from one of the world's best-loved romance authors.

Mills & Boon are proud to bring back these sought after titles, now reissued in beautifully matching volumes and presented as one cherished collection.

Don't miss these unforgettable titles, coming next month:

Title #9   WISH WITH THE CANDLES
Title #10 BRITANNIA ALL AT SEA

Available wherever
Mills & Boon books are sold

Available from WH Smith, John Menzies, Forbuoys, Martins, Tesco, Asda, Safeway and other paperback stockists.

One to Another

A year's supply of Mills & Boon® novels— absolutely FREE!

Would you like to win a year's supply of heartwarming and passionate romances? Well, you can and they're FREE! Simply complete the missing word competition below and send it to us by 28th February 1997. The first 5 correct entries picked after the closing date will win a year's supply of Mills & Boon romance novels (six books every month—worth over £150). What could be easier?

PAPER	B A C K	WARDS
ARM		MAN
PAIN		ON
SHOE		TOP
FIRE		MAT
WAIST		HANGER
BED		BOX
BACK		AGE
RAIN		FALL
CHOPPING		ROOM

Please turn over for details of how to enter ☞

How to enter...

There are ten missing words in our grid overleaf. Each of the missing words must connect up with the words on either side to make a new word—e.g. PAPER-BACK-WARDS. As you find each one, write it in the space provided, we've done the first one for you!

When you have found all the words, don't forget to fill in your name and address in the space provided below and pop this page into an envelope (you don't even need a stamp) and post it today. Hurry—competition ends 28th February 1997.

**Mills & Boon® One to Another
FREEPOST
Croydon
Surrey
CR9 3WZ**

Are you a Reader Service Subscriber?　　　Yes ❑　　No ❑

Ms/Mrs/Miss/Mr　_____

Address　_____

_____

_____ Postcode _____

One application per household.

You may be mailed with other offers from other reputable companies as a result of this application. If you would prefer not to receive such offers, please tick box.　❑

mps
MAILING
PREFERENCE
SERVICE

DMA

C496
A